HEART OF MISSISSIPPI

*Hot sultry nights with delicious docs—
in the heart of Mississippi...*

Kelsey and China Davis grew up with dark secrets
that rocked their once steady family foundations.
While China wants to stay in Golden Shores,
Kelsey can't wait to leave...

But neither sister expects to meet the two
gorgeous docs who have come to Golden Shores
searching for a fresh start. And once the fireworks
begin it's not long before pulses are racing and
temperatures are rising!

**The first story in Susan Carlisle's
Heart of Mississippi duet**

THE DOCTOR WHO MADE HER LOVE AGAIN

**is also available this month
from Mills & Boon® Medical Romance™**

Dear Reader

Small beach towns have always held a fascination for me. I've often wondered what it would be like to live in one year-round, to watch the crowds come and go, or to have seventy-degree weather when others are living in zero during the winter months. What I *haven't* wanted to experience is a hurricane, which is also part of residing along the Gulf Coast. Still, people choose to live and love in these towns where they might lose everything to Mother Nature.

My characters, Jordon and Kelsey, are a couple of these people. Kelsey has lived in the same tiny town all her life. She wants out. In fact that's all she can think about. Jordon has moved back to town after being gone for a number of years. It's the one place where he feels at home. Each sees living in Golden Shores from a vastly different perspective. Only through adversity do they manage to understand how the other feels and find happiness together.

I hope you enjoy Jordon and Kelsey's story, and the touch of sunshine the Gulf Coast brings to the story.

I love to hear from my readers. You can contact me at www.SusanCarlisle.com

Susan

THE MAVERICK WHO RULED HER HEART

BY
SUSAN CARLISLE

First published in Great Britain 2014
by Mills & Boon, an imprint of Harlequin (UK) Limited,
Eton House, 18-24 Paradise Road, Richmond, Surrey, TW9 1SR

© 2014 Susan Carlisle

ISBN: 978-0-263-24393-2

Harlequin (UK) Limited's policy is to use papers that are natural,
renew____ in
sustain____ ___form
to the

Printe___
by CP

Susan Carlisle's love affair with books began when she made a bad grade in maths in the sixth grade. Not allowed to watch TV until she'd brought the grade up, she filled her time with books and became a voracious romance reader. She has 'keepers' on the shelf to prove it. Because she loved the genre so much she decided to try her hand at creating her own romantic worlds. She still loves a good happily-ever-after story.

When not writing Susan doubles as a high school substitute teacher, which she has been doing for sixteen years. Susan lives in Georgia with her husband of twenty-eight years and has four grown children. She loves castles, travelling, cross-stitching, hats, James Bond and hearing from her readers.

Recent titles by Susan Carlisle:

Dedication

To Nick
Your mother loves you.

Praise for
Susan Carlisle:

CHAPTER ONE

JORDON KING COULDN'T decide if he was repulsed or fascinated by the tall, blonde woman with the spiked hair flit-
ting from one table to the next.

She greeted, smiled at and hugged each man as she
worked her way around the tables surrounding the dance
floor of the Beach Hut Bar and Grill in Golden Shores,
Mississippi. Maybe his issue was that she hadn't given any
attention to him. No, that wouldn't be the reason. Women
just weren't on his agenda right now. Getting his professional life back in order was.

Taking another draw on his drink, he placed the bottle
on the bar. What had it been? Fifteen years since he'd been
in the Beach Hut? Then he'd been underage and sneaking in with a fake ID. He surveyed the rustic room with
high wooden beams darkened from cigarette smoke before the no-smoking ban had been instituted. Very little
had changed, bringing back both good and bad memories
of the place.

Mark, one of his new colleagues at Golden Shores Regional Hospital, remarked as he looked toward the woman,
"Well, it looks like *she's* having a good time tonight."

"Yeah, it looks that way," Jordon said on a droll note.

"So, how do you like working and living in Golden
Shores?" Mark asked.

Jordon chuckled. "Well, I've not been here but two days, but so far so good. Thanks for the invite out tonight."

"No problem. I thought it might be a good way for you to meet a few people from the hospital."

That was the only reason Jordon had agreed to attend. Even in a small hospital there were people in departments he would never meet if it wasn't for some event like this. He watched as the blonde made a graceful movement, shifting one hip this way and then another as she made her way through the tight spaces between chairs toward the bar. There was something about her...

"Okay, everyone," the man on the stage said into the microphone. "It's time to get this party really started."

"For this next song I want you to find someone you either don't know well or don't know at all and bring them to the dance floor. Let's mix things up."

The blonde had been coming toward the bar and made a detour around a group, talking. It brought her out of the last set of chairs directly in front of him as the last of the instructions was given. Her gaze met his.

Never breaking their connection, she stepped up to him and said, "I don't know you. Want to dance?"

Even in the din her voice sounded low and raspy, like that of one of those old-time movie stars. Her eyes, which were almost too large for her face, watched him with an intensity that made him feel uncomfortable, as if daring him to turn her down.

Jordon shook his head.

She gave him a come-hither smile, crooked her index finger and beckoned him on. Had he met her before?

"No, thank you."

She stepped closer. "Oh, come on. It's impolite not to

accept someone's invitation to dance. Besides, you're the only guy in the place I don't know."

Maybe not. She didn't seem to know him. The woman really was a tease. Maybe the only way to get rid of her was to agree. He took another swig from his bottle and set it down, then nodded. Her smile turned brilliant, as if he'd given her the greatest gift. She headed for the dance floor and he followed.

This time he had an up-close view of her moving among the tangle of chairs and people. Her jeans fitted her perfectly, clinging to every single curve.

By the time he'd reached the dance floor, she was already turning to face him and starting to dance. Jordon joined her as she backed into the crowd and they were swallowed up. He was definitely more fascinated than repulsed when her hands went over her head and her eyes closed as she moved to the beat of the music. The woman was enjoying herself. She didn't need him there but he couldn't seem to turn away.

Dancing wasn't generally his thing but he did what he could not to embarrass himself. At one point she came out of her trance long enough to open her eyes and move into the light. He managed to catch a glimpse of her deep brown eyes. She jumped, startled for a second, then she gave him a weak smile. Where had all the earlier brightness gone?

One song died and the next one was building when she thrust out her hand and said, "I'm Kelsey."

She said the name as if she expected him to recognize it. He'd live in Golden Shores once for a short time as a teenager so maybe he should know her. He took her hand in his. It was warm, soft and small. Seconds later it slipped from his when a tall guy about the same age as him caught her attention. She turned to speak to him.

Jordon was forgotten just that quickly.

Who was that guy?

Kelsey had been racking her brains all night, trying to figure out why he looked so familiar. He leaned casually against the bar. With a solid appearance, trim hips and thick hair, he was by far the best-looking man in the place. She noticed him a number of times looking her direction with a censorious glare. One so familiar during her youth.

Dying of thirst, she'd managed to make her way to the bar. As the party planner and therefore designated hostess of the event, she'd spent most of her time making sure everyone was having a good time, especially the honoree and retiring employee, Patrice.

As if fate had taken her by the hand and led her astray, she arrived at the bar just as the emcee announced the dance. Her gaze locked with Mr. Handsome Glare.

She blurted out, "Do you want to dance?"

What had she been thinking? That was just it, she hadn't been thinking. To her surprise, and after major coaxing on her part, he'd agreed. She always loved to dance and, as if someone above was smiling down on her, they were playing her favorite song.

Out on the dance floor, where the light was brighter, she turned and looked at him. Her breath caught.

J-man.

That's all she knew him as. As a kid the name had sounded cool, maybe a little dangerous.

A ripple of nervousness went through her. Grateful she was dancing so that it didn't show, she kept moving after her initial falter. She'd never expected to see him again. Had grieved for him for months when he'd left without saying goodbye. In the middle of many lonely nights she'd fantasized about him returning to Golden Shores. Those had been preteen dreams. Long given up and forgotten. Still, the yellow plastic ring he'd given her lay in her jewelry box. What was he doing back here?

When she'd last seen him he'd been a thin seventeen-year-old with long hair that he'd pulled back at the nape of his neck. He had been her brother Chad's best friend, the one he'd gotten into trouble with.

For one stunned moment she looked into his eyes. A ripple of disappointment ran through her. He didn't recognize her. How could he not? He been everything to her at one time. But she'd only been one of his friends' little sisters. Someone they had to shoo out of the room when they got ready to talk. Still, it hurt that he didn't know her.

Kelsey glanced at him a couple of times. He wasn't the best dancer on the floor but he was making an effort. He wore a conservative shirt and khaki slacks. His jaw held a hint of five o'clock shadow that disrupted the perfect appearance.

As the song ended, Luke from the business office grabbed her arm and asked her a question. When she turned around J-man was gone.

Was he still going by that name? She couldn't imagine that he was. That label didn't suit him anymore. Searching the room, she saw his back as he headed out the door. Well, that was that, she probably wouldn't see him again. Maybe he was just a late summer tourist or, better yet, a figment of her imagination. Still, a sadness she didn't want to examine came over her.

On Monday morning Kelsey entered her office on the second floor of the hospital.

"Great party," Molly said.

Molly had been Kelsey's office colleague, roommate, and best friend since the eighth grade. "Thanks. It was a good one. I'll miss Patrice but I'm proud she has this chance."

"Yeah, she's been wanting to leave town since her divorce. The new job is perfect for her."

Kelsey wished she was the one leaving. She'd been trying to get out of Golden Shores for what seemed like forever. Away from her parents and the youthful reputation she couldn't quit shake clear of. If she landed the job at the hospital in Atlanta then they would be throwing her a party, hopefully in the next few weeks. She'd be free, with a clean slate.

"Hey, Kelsey." Marsha, a floor nurse, stuck her head in the door. "You're still doing the diabetic class this morning, aren't you? We've had a couple of calls about it."

"I am."

"The new hospitalist is going to stop by and introduce himself."

Kelsey wrinkled up her nose. "Who is it again?"

"Dr. King."

"Okay. I'll be on the lookout for him."

When Marsha left Kelsey said, "I guess a good nutritionist's work is never done."

Molly laughed. "I guess you're right."

Kelsey settled into the chair behind her desk and reviewed the patients she needed to speak to before they were discharged that day. She didn't have the most popular job with the patients but it was a necessary one. No one liked being told what they could or couldn't eat.

"Have you heard anything about this new doctor?" Kelsey asked. Not that it really mattered. She planned on being gone soon enough that it wouldn't affect her one way or another what type of person he was.

"All I've heard is that he's supposed to be excellent. I do know they didn't have to hunt him, he came looking for the position."

· "Here? I wonder why? We certainly aren't a hotbed of cutting-edge medical care."

Molly looked at her. "Not everyone feels a need to live somewhere else, be at the cutting edge. Some of us are perfectly fine living with the sand, sea, and surf."

As a child Kelsey had been also. Now all she wanted was to put the ugly memories behind her. But she couldn't do that if she stayed in Golden Shores. She'd tried. She acted out to forget. "Still mad at me about applying for the job?"

"Yeah, can't you tell?"

"I may not get it."

"You'll get it and I'll be stuck with another office mate, be looking for a new roommate." Molly looked at her. "But I won't be finding a new best friend."

"I love you too, Moll."

"It's mutual." A second later she whirled round again. "Oh, I forgot to mention the word around the hospital is that the new doc is gorgeous. There's already a betting pool started on who he'll ask out first. Nancy in the business office, Charlotte in the lab, or you."

"Really?" Kelsey couldn't seem to live down the good-time-girl rep she'd gained as a high-school and college student. It was hard to convince people who had known her during those times to take her seriously now. She wanted to go somewhere she could start afresh.

"Yeah. I'm putting my money on you. I need a new bathing suit so do what you can to help me out."

"I don't think so." Both woman mentioned were very attractive and seemed to make a point of meeting and dating the newest and most attractive men at the hospital, from the emergency crew to the administration office to the latest unattached doctor. Kelsey had moved past those fun and games.

Kelsey checked the large round clock on the wall and picked up the folder she'd laid out the night before that included pamphlets and handouts for the diabetes class.

"Got to go. We going to meet for lunch?"

"Sure. Whichever one of us gets to the table under the tree first claims it."

"Will do."

Late September beside the coast made it pleasant to eat outside. She and Molly, along with other staff members, fought over the coveted table under the large oak tree where the sun wouldn't beam down on them at noon. The other tables and chairs placed around the area weren't always as lucky.

Kelsey gathered her folder to her chest and went out the door. "Later."

Jordon drove up Main Street on his way to the hospital. He remembered the road well. He'd traveled it hundreds of times with his parents. As an only child he'd done almost everything with them.

Golden Shores hadn't changed much through the years. It was still a sleepy beach town that grew even more relaxed after the summer crowd had gone home. The storefronts were neat and in good repair. Baskets of late summer flowers, blooming yellow, red and blue, hung from the light poles at each intersection. This small insignificant town had been the last place he'd felt like he'd had a real home.

Pulling his SUV into the palm-lined drive of the hospital and following the signs to the designated doctors' parking lot, he found an open spot. Stepping out of the vehicle, he inhaled deeply. The spicy scent of salt filled his nostrils.

After spending so many years in snow during the winter, it was going to be nice to live here.

Jordon rolled his wrist and checked his watch. He was due for a meeting in twenty minutes. Last week he'd spent an entire day in Personnel, being issued his ID and getting acquainted with hospital procedures. Thank goodness he had no plans to ever leave so he'd not have to sit through one of those again.

With a quirk to his lips he punched in the number he'd been given for the doctors' entrance. He'd left the high-tech world of a large northern Virginia hospital where swiping a card for entry was the norm to the simple but effective push-button code.

Twenty minutes and two wrong turns later, he found the education classroom he was looking for. He stopped and double-checked the plaque by the door. This was the correct place.

Inside, a soft raspy voice said, "Today I'm going to be sharing some tips on how to eat well and at the same time tasty."

Looking into the room through the open door, he saw a dozen or so people sitting in chairs arranged in rows.

A man almost as round as he was tall said in a gruff voice. "All I can tell is that I can have a half a head of lettuce and nothing about that is tasty."

Everyone in the room laughed.

The voice responded, "Now, Mr. Franklin. You know that should only be a quarter of a head."

Again everyone chuckled.

Jordon stepped into the room and came to a jerking halt. The woman from the party was standing in front of the room. It was her voice he'd heard.

They stared at each other. She looked very familiar for some reason. He'd thought about her a couple of times since their meeting, trying to figure out where he knew her from. Could she be one of Chad's sisters? What if she was? Would she recognize him?

What he could remember of the youngest was that she had been around all the time. She'd been sweet, cute even, but way too young. He'd thought then, if you were just a little older...

Today her hair lay along her head in a boyish cut. And she wore bangs, pink and black glasses with polka dots on them, a simple hot-pink shirt and black slacks. Above her shoulders she seemed to come from a more unconventional world and below them from a conservative one.

So Miss Goodtime was the nutritionist. She seemed to recover from her surprise quicker than he did. "Uh, can I help you? If you're looking for the dietetic class, this is the place."

"Then I'm in the right place."

She waved a hand in the direction of an empty seat. "Then please join us." Her words sounded calm but from the slight tremor of her hand he could tell his appearance had flustered her.

"Thanks. I'm Dr. Jordon King."

At the sound of her hiss his head jerked up to meet her gaze. Her face had paled. What was going on?

He looked out at the group, hoping to give her time to recover from whatever the problem was. "I'm the hospitalist who will be caring for you if you're ever admitted. I hope that doesn't happen but I'll be here if you need me. I'm going to stay for the class so if you have any questions just let me know."

He took a chair behind the last person in the room and settled in. It had been a long time since he'd had time to sit through a presentation on diet and nutrition. It would be a nice refresher.

Despite having been put off by the demeanor of the woman at the front of the room's at the Beach Hut the other night, he found her professional and competent during her presentation of what to eat and portion control. She asked if there were any questions. A number of hands shot up.

She pointed to a balding man about halfway back and said, "Mr. Rawlins."

"Can I ever have cake?"

"In moderation only. Think birthdays and special occasions. Not nightly with ice cream."

There were groans around the room but she smiled. "Look, I'm not the bad guy here. Diabetes is. We're talking about a lifestyle change."

That's just what Jordon was doing. He would never have dreamt that he'd be back in Golden Shores. He had been on the fast track up the professional ladder. Had even been touted as possibly the youngest chief of staff, but backing his girlfriend and partner hadn't only cost Jordon his job but his credibility, his self-respect and his confidence in his ability to judge character. He planned to regain all of that in Golden Shores. This was his chance to start over with a clean slate. The woman's chuckle brought him back to the present. He didn't even know her full name. As soon as the class was over he was going to find out.

"Maybe that's a better question for Dr. King."

He jerked his gaze to hers. "I'm sorry, I missed that."

"Daydreaming in my class, Doc?"

All the class turned to look at him.

"Just for a sec. My apologies. Now, what was the question?" He stood and looked around the room expectantly.

"I would like to know," a woman of about thirty asked in a quiet voice, "if there's a chance that I might come off insulin."

"It depends on what type of diabetes you have. Some

people can control the disease with weight, others can take a pill and others require injections. Speak to your doctor and let him or her know that you would like to try."

The woman smiled at him and said, "Thanks, Doctor."

The speaker drew the group's attention again.

"That's all for today unless someone else has a question." No one said anything. "Then I'll see you all next week. Please bring your list of what you ate for review. Thanks for coming."

Everyone stood and gathered their belongings. Jordon moved to the front as people headed toward the rear. When he reached the woman she was speaking to one of the attendees and he waited. When the final person was out the door he said, "This is the second time we've met and I still don't know your full name."

A look he would have called disappointment if he didn't know better flashed through her eyes. Should he know her? He'd not kept in touch with anyone who still lived in Golden Shores except Chad, and he no longer lived here.

"I'm Kelsey Davis. Hospital nutritionist." She started picking up the papers on the podium in front of her.

Davis. Maybe she was one of Chad's sisters? But which one? Then again, Davis was a common name: there were a lot of them in the world. Surely more than one family in Golden Shores had the name Davis.

"Nice to meet you, Kelsey. I look forward to working with you."

"Hey, Kelsey." A man stuck his head inside the door.

He and Kelsey looked at him.

"Hey, Mike," Kelsey said with a smile.

"I'm sorry to interrupt," the young man, who had blond hair and the build of a weight lifter, said.

"Not a problem. I'm on my way out."

The man stepped into the room. As Jordon left he heard the man say, "Are we still on for tonight?"

Kelsey had never been more surprised than when the man from the party turned up in her classroom. More startling than that was the fact that J-man was the doctor she'd be working with regularly. She gotten over being nervous around boys along ago, but for some reason J-man, uh, Jordon made her stomach queasy. He'd been her first love. Now he didn't even remember her!

She'd not seen him since her brother and he had gotten arrested. Right before they had both disappeared. Jordon had been part of the reason her brother, Chad, had issues with their father. Only Chad had never come home. Part of the blame for why her family had become so screwed up was rooted in that long-ago night.

Where Chad was concerned she had a love/hate relationship with him. She'd adored him. He'd been the oldest to her youngest and she'd idolized him. When he'd left without saying anything to her she'd been devastated. As the years had gone by she'd grown to resent him too. Because of him her once happy life had crumbled and she couldn't seem to get all the pieces back into place. At least with China that was starting to happen. She wasn't even sure she ever wanted to make the effort with regards to her parents. Getting out of Golden Shores, closing the door on the past had always sounded like the best answer.

Now J-man was back as a doctor. Life really was crazy. If it hadn't been time for her to leave town before, it surely was now. Until the new job came through, she'd stay out of his way as much as possible.

At noon Kelsey carried her tray from the cafeteria to the table where Molly waited under the tree. She slid into the open spot next to her.

"Hey, how'd it go this morning? Did you meet the new doctor? He's the talk of the hospital." Molly picked up her sandwich.

"That's not a hard thing to be. This hospital isn't that big and most of the people who work here have known each other most of their lives." Except Jordon, who had no idea who she was or the part he'd played in her young life.

"So are you going to tell me what you think about him?" Molly studied her.

Kelsey was well aware of who Dr. King was. Too aware. She didn't want Molly to know everything she thought about him. "He's nice enough and seems to know his medicine."

Molly put down her fork and looked at Kelsey like she had two heads. "That's all you've got to say? Kelsey Davis, I've known you since middle school and that's the least I've ever heard you say about a male. He must have really done something wrong."

Molly had no idea. She'd moved to town the next summer. About Chad and how she'd felt about J-man were the only secrets she'd ever kept from Kelsey. "Okay, okay. What do you want? That he's the best-looking man I've seen. Dark hair, hazel eyes, shoulders from here to eternity and a butt to die for!"

Molly giggled. "That's more like it but I detect a note of cynicism. Problem?"

"No. He just reminds me of someone I used to know."

"Someone you didn't like."

She'd liked him too well. "I liked the person just fine but it was during a bad time in my life."

"Hello, beautiful ladies. Mind if I join you."

Kelsey looked up to see Adam standing there. He worked in X-ray and had gone to school with her and Molly.

"Sure," Molly said. She nodded toward the other bench.

* * *

Jordon followed Mark to the only outside table available. He took a spot opposite him, gave the food on his tray a dubious look and made a mental note to remember to bring his lunch as often as he could.

A loud burst of laughter came from the table to their left. Jordon knew without looking that Kelsey Davis was there. He'd noticed her along with another blonde with long hair, and he wasn't surprised to see a man sitting with them. Was every man drawn to her?

His mother had the same personality. People gravitated toward her, especially men. His father had proudly said more than once that "his Margaret was the life of any party." Jordon had loved to hear her laugh. It had always made him smile. Until that night when the sound had woken him. Her tinkling lilt had drawn him to her until he'd realized she'd been talking suggestively on the phone to a man other than his father.

He glared in the direction of the other table.

"Kelsey and Molly seem to be having a good time. They must be up to something."

"Up to something?" Jordon took a bite of his oven-baked chicken.

"Yeah, they're always planning a party or some outing or something."

Jordon grunted acknowledgement.

"You'll like working with Kelsey. She's a lot of fun."

"What's her story?"

Mark shrugged. "I don't know. The usual, I guess. Grew up here, lives here and will die here."

"You knew her before you started working here?"

"Yeah. We went to high school together. She has a bit of a reputation as a party girl. She enjoys having a good time but I never hear anyone saying anything but good things about her now."

"Does her family still live around here?"

"I don't know. Why?"

"She looks so familiar. I used to know some Davises, I just thought she might be kin to them."

"Why don't you ask her?"

"Maybe I will." He glanced at Kelsey's table again. But this woman *couldn't* be the young girl he'd once known. She giggled at something that had been said then turned, meeting his gaze. Time ground to a halt as they stared at each other before he forced his attention back to his unimpressive meal.

Either way, she wasn't someone he needed to get involved with.

That evening he was walking toward his car when he saw Kelsey getting into an aging small compact that didn't fit the persona he'd seen so far. It was nothing flashy, as he would've expected. She pulled out of her spot and passed him with little more than a glance. How could he be so aware of her when she didn't seem to even notice him?

CHAPTER TWO

MIDMORNING THE NEXT day Jordon's cell phone rang while he was familiarizing himself with some paperwork. Tapping the icon, he said, "Dr. King here."

"This is the E.R. clerk. You're needed here."

"On my way."

Rushing down the stairs, he made one turn and headed along a short hallway. He grinned as he walked. The last hospital he'd been affiliated with had been so large it had taken him five minutes to go from his office to the E.R.

He stepped up to the circular desk and said to the person sitting there, "I'm Dr. King. You paged me."

"You're needed in exam room three."

He look around.

The clerk pointed and said, "Down that way."

"Thanks."

Voices came from behind the closed curtain that hung across a metal rod. This was another reminder that he'd left a more modern facility behind. There the patient examination rooms would have had been enclosed. Golden Shores might not be up to date on their buildings but by all accounts the hospital provided excellent medical care and had a clean report as far as any medical malfeasance was concerned. He had no intention of letting what had happened in Washington occur again. He'd been embarrassed and publicly humiliated on too many levels for one lifetime. He'd make sure this time not to get involved with anyone or anything looking remotely illegal.

One of the voices coming from the other side of the curtain sounded familiar. Pulling the striped material back, he saw a woman who looked to be in her late seventies lying on the gurney. Kelsey sat next to the bed and held the older woman's hand.

Was she destined to turn up everywhere he went?

He raised a brow in her direction and made an effort to concentrate on the patient. Before he could ask a question a nurse rushed in.

"Dr. King, here's the chart."

He looked at the front page and said, "So what seems to be the problem Mrs.?" He glanced at the chart again. "Ritch."

"Young man, you may call me Martha."

He raised a brow. "Okay, Martha, what brought you in today?"

"I was playing bridge, as I always do over at Edith Hutchinson's house, and I just blacked out."

"Did you fall out of the chair?" he asked, concerned the she might have a concussion.

"More like slipped, Myrtice said as I was being put into the ambulance. Which is going to cost me my entire war pension."

Kelsey patted the woman's arm. "Now, Martha, that isn't the important thing. We'll take care of it."

Jordon cringed. That was what his lover and partner had said just before they'd arrested her for insurance fraud. He wouldn't take a chance on being involved in anything like that again. Jordon gave Kelsey a questioning look. Why was she here? She returned an unwavering gaze. Had she seen him wince at her words?

"Martha is one of my diabetic patients. She asked the nurse to call me."

He nodded. "So did you feel like your blood sugar had dropped?"

The woman hung her head. "I knew when I ate Sally's petits fours that I'd be in trouble."

"Martha! We've talked about this!" Kelsey exclaimed.

"I know, hon. But there's nothing like Sally's petits fours. You can't eat just one."

Jordon cleared his throat. "Well, then, young lady..."

Martha giggled. Kelsey smiled, which captivated him.

A few seconds later Martha made a huffing noise. "You do know I'm the patient, don't you?"

Jordon blinked and looked at her. "I'm well aware you are my patient. And apparently you don't follow doctor's orders. I'd like to keep you overnight and give you a good checkup just to make sure we have your blood-sugar level back in line." He looked at Kelsey. "I also would like Ms. Davis to give you a refresher course on what to eat and not eat. Just in case there's something that wasn't covered."

He noticed Kelsey stiffen but he wasn't sure why.

"I understand," Marsha said, with just enough humility to make him believe she might be more cautious about the number of petits fours she ate in the future.

"All right, I'll get the paperwork started to have you admitted."

"At least that isn't committed," Martha said.

Jordon chuckled. Martha reminded him of Ms. Olson, one of the patients he'd had to leave behind in DC. He'd miss her and what he'd worked so hard to build.

"I don't think your infraction was that serious but you can't keep eating petits fours. The nurse will be in to see about getting you admitted to the floor. I'll check in on you this evening before I leave."

Jordon pushed the curtain back and stepped out into the large open space of the ER. Before the curtain fell back into place Kelsey joined him.

"May I speak to you a moment, Doctor? In private."

She didn't wait for him to respond before she started out the double doors of the E.R. Left little choice, he followed her. She glanced back as she rounded a corner but continued on. He had a nice view of her high tight behind incased in blue pants that defined it to perfection. When he saw her again, she was standing beside a door. She pushed it open and entered as he approached.

Kelsey had no idea what she'd been thinking when Jordon had entered the small consultation room. Suddenly there hadn't been enough space or air. She hadn't been rational, she'd been too angry. She couldn't afford anyone to imply she didn't do her job well. He had inferred just that.

The chance of getting the job in Atlanta was far too important. If that got back to the administration of the new hospital she'd never have a chance at the position. It was hard enough to overcome the past, she didn't need anything else to stand in her way. Some of the administration staff had known her as a kid and still had a hard time seeing her as a responsible employee.

The second the door clicked closed Kelsey turned to face him and took a step closer, putting only a foot between them. Looking up at the tall and rather large man, she questioned her decision-making. He gazed at her with complete innocence, which fueled her ire to the point she gritted her teeth to stop herself from doing something far more stupid and unethical.

"Back there it sounded as if you might be implying that I hadn't done my job," she hissed. "That I am responsible when a patient doesn't follow dietary directions outside this hospital. I assure you that I instruct to the best of my ability but I cannot make anyone do what they don't want to do."

To her amazement, he looked surprised, maybe slightly annoyed.

"I didn't mean to imply—"

"Whether you did or didn't, it came out that way. You've not been here long enough to make any assumptions about my work. I don't need there to be any insinuations or suggestions that I don't do my job well."

"I didn't do either!"

. "Just know I don't appreciate what you said. You're the new guy here and I'm going to let it go this time. If this happens again, just know we will be having another discussion. We have to work together and I'll be professional and I expect you to be the same."

He stepped toward her.

She'd made an uncalculated mistake. He stood squarely between her and the door. She wanted out and he was as formidable as a Stonehenge boulder.

"Are you finished?" he growled, his eyes narrowing.

Kelsey forced herself not to gulp.

"I don't know what you think I did," he continued, "but I assure you I didn't say that you were responsible. I know how rumors and unsubstantiated statements can damage a career. I would never do that to anyone. As for not appreciating something, I haven't allowed someone to harangue me in this manner since my mother caught me stealing money out of her purse when I was a kid. So, Ms. Davis, you can give it a rest."

He turned, jerked the door open and was gone before Kelsey could form a parting word. She scowled at the closed door.

* * *

Jordon drove home down Bay Road toward the house he'd rented in a "snowbird" deal. He would live there through the winter months while he looked for a place to buy. As a kid, his house had been a part of a subdivision located further inland. He'd always envied his friends at school who lived on the water so that was where he planned to get a place. When he'd returned to town he'd decided against one of the large condos on the ocean side and had opted for a place on the bay.

Pulling the SUV into the white crushed-shell drive and beside the one-floor bungalow, he turned the engine off and looked out at the water beyond. The sea grass waved gently in the wind. Yes, he'd done the right thing by coming back here. Not all the memories were great but the ones before his parents' divorce outnumbered those afterwards.

Hardy, his chocolate Labrador, barked his welcome as he climbed out. The dog already had a stick in his mouth, waiting for Jordon to play.

"Hey, boy." He leaned down and gave the dog a good pat on the side. "Let me change and we'll go to the water."

Opening the door to the house, he stepped straight into the kitchen area. The place had been built in the sixties and little had changed. Dark paneling, overstuffed furniture with wooden armrests and laminated floors in an unappealing green didn't deviate from the traditional décor of the times. The house wasn't attractive but it was clean and functional. The only concession made to change was the large TV on a stand in the corner. Jordon didn't plan to miss a single Washington Redskins' football game if he could help it.

He pulled his knit shirt over his head as he went down the hall to the larger of the two bedrooms. Throwing his shirt in the corner, he pulled on a well-worn T-shirt. It was nice not to have to wear a dress shirt and tie to work. The causal, more laid-back coastal lifestyle suited him just fine. Best of all, no white lab coat was required. Shucking his tan slacks and stepping into his favorite jeans, he pulled them into place, zipped and buttoned them.

Not bothering with shoes, he'd take his chance on not getting sand spears in his feet just to feel grass between his toes. He walked across the cool floor back to the kitchen to pour himself glass of tea. He'd always like sugar sweet tea and that was something he couldn't get north of the Mason-Dixon line. Back in the Deep South, if he asked for tea, it came sweet. One more perk about moving home, and that was just what he'd done—come home. He didn't plan to ever move again.

With glass in hand he called, "Come on, boy, let's go play fetch."

Despite it being late September, the weather was still plenty warm. Hardy pranced at Jordon's heels as he strolled to the dock where an Adirondack chair waited. Sitting facing west with a sigh of pleasure, he waited for the sun to set. Hardy dropped his stick to the wooden planks of the pier beside the chair and whimpered.

"Okay, boy. I'll play with you if you promise to watch the sunset with me." Jordon threw the stick out into the water. In a flash, Hardy sprang off the dock. Paddling, he reached the stick, grasped it in his mouth and headed back. Once on shore again, he shook himself and came running back to Jordon.

"Good boy." He patted the wet, wiggling dog and willingly took the shower of water when the dog shook himself again.

Hardy barked and Jordon sent the wood out over the water again. Hardy didn't hesitate before jumping from the dock and swimming toward his stick. A blaze of color caught Jordon's eye, pulling his attention away from the dog. A woman in a large pink-brimmed hat on her head strolled out onto a pier a couple of doors away. Jordon forgot the sunset and Hardy as he watched the woman pull off her cover-up and let the mesh jacket drop to the planks.

Yes, undeniably he was going to enjoy living here.

The hand with his drink in it stopped in midair as he studied her. She had smooth curves in all the right places. The tiny blue bikini she wore accented them perfectly. As she turned, then bent to adjust the lounge downward, he caught a glimpse of her face.

Kelsey Davis. How had he not recognized those curves from earlier? Maybe he'd been distracted by all that golden skin.

Did she live two doors down? Surely she was just visiting a friend.

As if she'd become aware of someone watching her, she glanced around. Her body stiffened the second she realized his gaze was on her. She hurriedly sat in the chair.

To his horror, Hardy came out of the water and didn't look right or left before making a beeline toward Kelsey's pier. As if in slow motion, Jordon stood and started moving as Hardy ran the length of the dock, dropped the stick beside Kelsey and shook himself. Water droplets filled the air, glistening in the early evening sunlight, to fall over Kelsey like rain.

Jordon ran and called Hardy, to no avail. He had made it to the entrance of her dock in time to hear Kelsey squeal then yelped when Hardy's wet tail ran across her thigh and up over her belly. In her effort to roll away from the dog, she toppled the lounge and fell to the pier. By the time he'd sprinted to the end of her dock, Kelsey lay on her side on the rough planks, pushing Hardy away, while the dog tried to poke his nose in her face.

"Hardy," he snapped.

The dog looked at him as if to say, Get your own girl.

Jordon chuckled.

"Are you laughing at me?" Kelsey's eyes had turned cavern dark in her anger. That emotion was familiar. He seemed to elicit it from her with little trouble.

"No, I'm just laughing at the picture you two make." Jordon grabbed Hardy's collar.

"It figures this monster would be yours."

He looked pointedly at her. "You don't like dogs?"

"I like dogs fine. I'm just not wild about showers given by them or sloppy kisses."

"I'll remember that."

Her eyes grew wide. Why had he said something so suggestive? He had no intention of sharing a shower with her, much less kissing her. She wasn't his type. Even if she had been, the sting of betrayal still smarted. It was best she remain on her dock and he on his.

Kelsey started to rise.

Jordon offered her a hand. "Here, let me help you."

After a second she took it and he tugged her upwards.

He sucked in a breath. As amazing as she'd looked from his dock, she was breathtaking up close. The bikini showed off most of her body but he still wanted to see more. Her breasts were full and high. His fingers itched to stroke them, just once.

"Can't you handle your dog?" Her eyes snapped as she glared at him.

"I guess he appreciates a pretty woman as well as the next male."

She squared her shoulders, which thrust her barely covered breasts upward. He couldn't help but stare.

"Surely you aren't flirting with me?"

Jordon couldn't pull his gaze away from the beauty before him. "What if I was?" he muttered. What had made him ask that? A half-naked woman had never made him lose his mind before. For heaven's sake, he was a doctor. Was his thirty-seconds-ago vow to keep his distance already going by the wayside?

Kelsey picked up the cover-up from the dock, giving him a fine view of her behind before she pulled the jacket on and tied it. "Don't."

Hardy bumped her leg. She leaned down and took his face in her hands. "So what's this guy's name?"

Jordon had to give her points for being a good sport. No other woman he'd known in the past or present would've taken Hardy's antics so well. "Hardy. As in Laurel and Hardy. Mr. Personality he is."

"You have beautiful eyes," she cooed.

How ridiculous was it to be jealous of his dog? Hardy seemed to melt like chocolate on a warm day under her ministrations. Jordon might have too, except he couldn't seem to get any positive attention from Kelsey.

"I had a dog almost just like you when I was a kid."

She stopped petting Hardy and straightened. It was as if her enthusiasm had suddenly waned. There was a sad note in her voice as if she'd remembered something she didn't want to. Had something happened to her dog when she'd been a kid? Wanting to change the subject, he asked, "So, do you live here?"

"Yeah."

"We're neighbors. I've got the place a couple houses over."

"Great," she said, with less gusto than he would have liked to hear. Why did it matter what she thought?

"Well, I guess we'll let you get back to your sunbathing or whatever you were doing. Come on, Hardy."

The dog looked from one to the other then sat beside Kelsey.

She said with a smirk on her lips, "I guess your dog likes me better."

Jordon picked up Hardy's stick and threw it in the direction of his dock. The dog jumped into the water.

"See you later, Kelsey," Jordon tossed over his shoulder smugly, as he walked up the dock toward the shore.

Back on his own dock, he threw the piece of wood two additional times for Hardy, in an effort to forget Kelsey only yards away. It didn't work. His attention kept slipping back to her. It wasn't just that she was a beautiful half-dressed woman within eyesight but Kelsey intrigued him on a number of levels. She was plain old-fashioned interesting. Something that women he was acquainted with weren't.

Hardy, finally worn out, lay down beside him. Jordon absently rubbed his ear. "Thank you for being such a turncoat."

The dog said nothing and Jordon continued to watch Kelsey as she read a book, the sunset no longer of interest. At dusk Kelsey folded her chair down, gathered her belongings and headed toward the house.

"Good night, Kelsey," Jordon said softly.

He stayed until the night swallowed up the last ray of light then made his way inside with Hardy at his heels. "I hope the view is as good every night," he said to Hardy, not sure if he meant of Kelsey or the sunset.

The next morning Kelsey tried her ignition switch one more time. Nothing. Was it just a dead battery or something more?

How was she going to get to work? Molly had a doctor's appointment and had left earlier. Great. It wouldn't look or sound good when her superiors were contacted by someone in Atlanta and they had her being late to work fresh in their memory. She needed a ride quickly. Looking two driveways over, she confirmed that the blue SUV was still sitting in the drive.

She grabbed her purse from the passenger seat, stuffed it under her arm and started in the direction of Jordon's bungalow. It would have been nice if one of the other houses around them was occupied but they were only used seasonally so she had no choice but to ask Jordon for help. She wasn't looking forward to asking him for a ride, but she had little choice unless she walked, and she would be late for sure if she did that.

She stepped up to Jordon's door. Her hand faltered before she knocked. Barking preceded the door being pulled open. Behind the screen door, wearing no shirt, stood Jordon.

"Well, good morning," he drawled in an exaggerated tone.

Why did the man manage to set her teeth on edge? Taking a deep breath, she said, "My car won't start. Can I get a ride with you?"

He grinned, "So what you're staying is you're not angry with me anymore."

"I knew you wouldn't be a gentleman about this."

Jordon clasped his hands over his heart. "That hurt. Of course I'll be glad to give you a ride." His grin grew and he pushed the screen door open and used his leg to block Hardy from exiting the house. "I'm almost ready. Want to come in and wait?"

Her gaze found his chest. "I'll just wait out by your SUV."

He shrugged and let the door slam. "Suit yourself."

The guy was so smug. What was it about her that made him so rude?

She'd been acutely aware of him behind her while she'd sat on the pier the previous evening. It had taken all her willpower not to glance behind her to see if he was watching her. She'd read the same three pages of her book five times and she still couldn't have told anyone what they'd been about. All she'd been able to think about had been what Jordon had been doing.

Refusing to give him the satisfaction of him knowing that he'd rattled her, she'd acted as unaffected by him as she'd been able. He'd completely ruined her plans for a relaxing evening. Wishing he would leave, she'd given up at dusk and packed her belongs. She had been grateful that he hadn't been sitting close enough to see her hands shake when she'd risen.

Had she heard "Good night, Kelsey" drift on the wind?

"Hey, you going to get in or daydream all morning?"

She blinked then focused on him. "I'm going to get in."

At the beep of the door being unlocked, she climbed into the vehicle and settled into the large comfortable seat. Jordon effortlessly took his spot behind the wheel. They didn't speak as he backed out of the drive and drove toward town. As they passed the blue house about a mile up the road Jordon commented, "I used to know a family that lived there. They were the Davises. Are you any kin to them?"

A sick feeling went through her. So he did remember. But there was no point in lying. "Yeah. Their daughter."

He jerked his head around to look at her.

"You might want to watch the road," she said.

"So you're one of Chad's sisters." He sounded utterly amazed.

"I am."

He nodded as if in thought. "Which one are you?"

She'd hung on his every word as a kid. She'd thought he'd been the be-all and end-all and he couldn't remember which one she was. That stung. "I'm the youngest one," she made herself say in a strong voice.

He pulled to the side of the road and turned to look at her. "So have you known all along who I was?"

"I recognized you while we were dancing."

"Why didn't you say something?"

She suddenly felt the need to defend herself. "I didn't even know your real name until you came into my class. You were always J-man to me. We need to get going or we'll be late."

He pulled the SUV back onto the road. "J-man. I've not been called that for years."

"Why did you move back?" Kelsey asked. There had to be something in particular to make anyone want to come back to Golden Shores.

The only indication he gave that her question might have disturbed him was the tightening of his hands on the steering wheel.

"It was time to make a change."

"But why here, of all places?"

"Because this is the last place I remember feeling like I belong," he said matter-of-factly.

Kelsey huffed. "And it's the one place I wish I didn't belong."

This conversation had gone way past a simple ride to the hospital. Kelsey was relieved when Jordon pulled the SUV into the hospital parking lot. She had to get out of there.

"Thanks for the ride," she said, opening the door of the SUV before Jordon had turned the engine off.

"Kelsey—"

She closed the door and headed for the employees' entrance, refusing to look back.

Answering questions about her family wasn't how she wanted to start her day. Jordon couldn't help but bring back unhappy memories. She missed Chad as much today as she had then. If she only knew if he was still alive.

Jordon watched as Kelsey entered the hospital and disappeared behind the metal outside door as if she'd pulled up the drawbridge. So she was Chad's sister. That sister. The one that he had wished he'd be around to see when she got older. Did she remember him as fondly as he remembered her?

Did she know where Chad was? Kelsey acted as if she didn't want to talk about anything having to do with her family. She'd not even looked at her parents' house when he'd driven by. He and Chad had been two unhappy teens who'd bonded and fueled each other's frustration. Leading up to his parents' divorce and afterward, he had been angry. Whatever his father had said, he'd done the opposite.

He'd started hanging out at the park with the wrong crowd, more to irritate his father than liking the kids who had been there. One night Chad Davis had shown up. He was a year younger but they'd seemed to hit it off. They'd started hanging around with each other at school, ditching classes together and otherwise becoming best friends. That had been until the night they'd been caught by the police, smoking dope.

Jordon climbed out of the SUV and slowly made his way inside. Did Kelsey know her brother was in the state prison not an hour away? When he'd visited Chad on the way to Golden Shores and told him about moving here, Chad had made Jordon promise that if he ever saw any of his family he wouldn't tell them where he was. At the time it was no big deal to make that promise. But now how long would he be able to honor that request? But trust, giving his word meant everything. Jordon wouldn't break his.

He'd certainly not wanted to discuss way he'd decided to move back to Golden Shores, with Kelsey or anyone else for that matter. Those events had been too painful. Shown how easily he'd been duped by someone he'd cared about. That had happened one too many times in his life. He would be careful about who he let his guard down to from now on.

In his office, he checked his messages. He was asked to be at a staff meeting at ten in the cafeteria. What was going on? Was some dignitary coming to town? He'd find out soon enough. There was just enough time to make rounds.

It was five minutes past ten when he entered the cafeteria. The room was packed so he stood against the wall. He hadn't been able to get there any sooner because Martha had kept asking him questions and telling him stories when he'd checked on her.

The CEO stood at the front of the room. "Most of you have been through this before, many of you more than once. Still, I want you to review your emergency procedures. In a few minutes you can get with your teams and update your contact numbers. The weather service isn't calling for the storm to hit here but we need to be prepared if it takes a turn our way. It's our job to work calmly and efficiently. Our community expects us to be here for them and we will be."

So they were preparing for a hurricane. Maybe he should have been watching the news instead of Kelsey last night.

"Dr. King?" He looked around the room.

Jordon gave the CEO a wave. "Here."

The CEO nodded in Jordon's direction. "I hate to put you on the ground running so quickly but you're to take over Dr. Richards's team. Everyone previously on Dr. Richards's team, please get together with Dr. King when we adjourn. I think that's all, folks. Check in with each other and keep your phones charged. On a positive closing note, we are going ahead with the hospital-wide low country boil picnic Saturday, unless the weather says something different."

Hospital picnic? He'd never been to one. The hospitals he'd trained in had been in metropolitan areas and far too large for such things. Another perk of living in a small town. A low country boil did sound good. He'd not been to one of those in a long time.

Having no idea who was on his team, he waited until he was approached by someone. Talk about being a fish out of water.

"Dr. King?" a balding man wearing a tie asked.

Jordon nodded. "Please, make it Jordon."

"I'm Jim. I work in the business office. I'll be handling the paperwork, communication and be your runner."

Jordon offered his hand. "Nice to meet you, Jim. So we are preparing for a hurricane?"

"Yeah, around here it isn't if we will have a hurricane but when."

"How many more are on our team?"

"Two more. Josh Little and Kelsey Davis."

Jordon almost groaned. She wouldn't like that any more than he did.

A tall man, dressed in nursing scrubs with golden hair and biceps that said he spent time in the gym daily, joined them.

"Hey, I'm Josh Little. I'll be your nurse."

The two men shook hands.

"I'm going to depend on you to keep me straight. I've never done this type of thing before," Jordon said.

"Nothing to it. Kelsey will be the boss," Josh said with a smile.

"Sorry I'm late. I was all the way across the room."

Jordon knew the voice that came from behind him.

He turned to look at her. She didn't appear any more enthusiastic about seeing him than he was to see her. "Glad you could join us, Kelsey. I understand you're the one who will tell me what to do."

She narrowed her eyes. "Our team does triage. You tell me which ones are the most urgent and I tag them. Josh handles care until you can see them. Jim will record everything."

"So where does this all happen?" Jordon looked at the group but the question was addressed to Kelsey.

"Our designated area is in the hospital lobby."

"What about supplies?" he asked.

"All that is taken care of. Housekeeping sets up and has the space ready to go if or when needed," Josh offered.

Jordon nodded his understanding. "Great. So all we need to do is exchange numbers?"

Kelsey said, "That's it." They all went through the process of telling each other their phone numbers.

"Who is responsible for doing all the calling?" Jordon asked.

"I do that," Jim stated.

Jordon looked at him and grinned. "So the plan here is to hope that I don't hear from you."

Jim smiled back. "That's the plan."

There was a buzz. "I've got to go. E.R. is paging me," Josh said.

"I've got to go too," Jim added.

As Kelsey turned to leave Jordon said, "Hey, Kelsey, will you tell me about the hospital picnic?"

She didn't look like she wanted to but she stopped. "It's held at the state park down on the beach. Food is provided and there are games. You know, the regular family stuff."

"You planning to attend?"

"I usually do."

"That didn't answer my question."

She looked at him for a second then said, "I haven't missed one in five years so I don't think I'll be missing this one."

"Mind if I tag along with you? I don't really know anyone."

It took her so long to answer he started to think she wasn't going to. Suddenly there was a look of triumph on her face.

"I have to be there early to set up. I'm on the committee."

"I don't mind going along and helping out."

"Good. I'm going to take you at your word. I'll pick you up a seven a.m. on Saturday. No, let me change that. You drive. You've got a bigger vehicle."

"Why do I think I've just been had?"

Kelsey grinned then walked off.

The weatherman had said the storm had stalled in the Gulf and wouldn't be coming ashore until early the next week. Saturday dawned sunny with a light breeze. The picnic was still on. Jordon pulled up into Kelsey's drive promptly at seven in the morning. He and Kelsey hadn't had much interaction in the last few days other than brief encounters over patients.

The door to her place opened. She stepped out and waved, indicating she needed him to come inside. He climbed out of the SUV and she called, "Hey, did you plan to sit there while I do all the work?"

"Sorry, I didn't know I was needed." He strolled toward the door. Kelsey had already disappeared inside again.

She pushed the door open and handed him a large box. "This needs to go, then come back and help me with the ice chests."

"Yes, ma'am."

Having stowed the box, he returned. The door wasn't open so he knocked and called through the screen door, "Kelsey?"

"Come on in."

She didn't wait for him to respond, disappearing down the hall.

Jordon entered. The interior was arranged very much like his place. The only thing different was that this bungalow had a feminine feel to it. Candles were arranged on the counter, bright throw blankets lay over the furniture and pictures of flowers adorned the walls.

"The coolers are next to the bar in the kitchen. I'll be there to help in a sec."

True to her word, she stepped into the room a few minutes later, wearing a tight T-shirt with something sparkling around the scooped neckline that gave him a hint of cleavage and cutoff jeans that showed off her legs to their best advantage. There was something raw and inviting about her. A woman who stood out in a crowd. He could see a touch of the young girl there too that he known so many years before.

Kelsey reached for a handle on one end of a large box cooler and he took the other. Together they carried it out. When they got to the rear of the SUV, they set it down while Jordon opened the doors.

"I'll take it from here." He lifted the cooler into the vehicle. "What have you got in this thing? Rocks?"

"Water balloons."

"Water balloons!"

"I'm in charge of the water-balloon fight."

"I'm glad I'm not signed up for that."

"You're too old," she quipped.

"How's that? My hair's not even gray yet."

"It's for the teenagers. That's how we get them to come to the picnic each year."

Jordon pushed the cooler further into the SUV. "Makes sense. Is that it?"

She turned toward the house. "Nope. There's another cooler."

"Why am I not surprised?"

Together they brought another cooler out to the SUV. "Just how were you planning to get these to the park if I hadn't come along?"

"Aw, I would have gotten one of the guys at work to help me."

That he wasn't shocked to hear. She seemed to always have some guy hanging around. Right now he wasn't much different but he'd keep his distance, if not in the physical sense the at least on an emotional level.

"Anything else?"

"I just have to get one more small cooler and a couple of bags. And my cake."

"Was I supposed to bring something?"

"No. Someone suggested we have a cake auction to raise money to help redecorate the children's wing. I was roped into baking one."

"I'll help you with the bags and you can handle the cake."

Ten minutes later they were in the SUV, headed toward town.

"Do you know where the park is?"

He gave her an incredulous look. "Yes. Remember I used to live here."

"That's right. I keep forgetting."

Something about the way she made that statement made him believe that wasn't true.

As he drove past her parents' home he watched out of the corner of his eye to see if she looked. Her focus remained straight ahead. He wanted to ask her if she knew where Chad was, what had happened after he'd left town, but today wasn't the right time. It would wait.

CHAPTER THREE

THE PARKING LOT already had a number of cars in it when they arrived.

Kelsey pointed. "See the white tent over there. If you could back up to it, we can unload easier."

Jordon did as instructed. Kelsey was out of the SUV and opening the back door before he moved the gearshift into park. A couple of guys he recognized came to help them. After unloading, Kelsey was still busy issuing orders as Jordon moved the SUV to a parking spot out of the way. He was locking up when he saw Kelsey's cake sitting on the floor of the passenger seat. She must have forgotten it. He picked it up and walked back across the parking lot to where she was helping set up tables.

"Kelsey," he called, "where do I need to put your cake?"

More than one person stopped what they were doing and looked at her.

A red hue covered her face and by the thrust of her chin she left no doubt she was not pleased with his question.

"Kelsey, you baked a cake?" one woman asked.

"The last one you put salt in instead of sugar," another commented with a grin.

"I thought you'd just buy one and put your name on it," the guy helping Kelsey put chairs around a table said with a chuckle.

Kelsey took a proud stance. "Hey, look, I can bake with the best of them I just choose not to on most occasions." She tossed her head and went back to work.

"I think we need all the cakes we can get for the auction," another woman offered. "Maybe the fact that the winner of the cake gets to share it with the baker will make Kelsey's the highest earner."

"Thank you, Carolyn. You're a true friend." Kelsey said, then looked around at the crowd. "Unlike everyone else."

Kelsey put the last chair around the table, stalked over to Jordon and all but snatched the cake out of his hands. "Thanks," she hissed.

"I didn't know you were hiding it," he said, for her ears only. "Sorry."

"Forget it."

Jordon had no idea her baking was such a sore point. Where she was concerned, he kept making mistakes. "Can I help with something?"

"We still need to put up the tables for the games." She pointed toward a woman with a blue ball cap on her head. "Pam over there will tell you what to do."

Jordon was a little disappointed she was fobbing him off on another person, but he didn't need to be spending any more time with her than he presently had. He'd had to fight the urge to jump in and defend her baking skills. She wouldn't have appreciated that and he was even more perplexed by the idea that he thought he should.

The hours flew by as he helped first Pam then Max and finally Roger to get the large burner and pots ready to cook the meal. At around ten, cars began arriving one after another. It was a family event, so kids showed up in all shapes and sizes. As the morning went on he only caught glimpses of Kelsey from a distance but he seemed to search her out every so often as if she was his to watch over. Which she certainly wasn't.

One time he saw her hugging a petite woman with shoulder-length brown hair. Kelsey smiled at the tall man who had a possessive arm around the woman's waist. Something about the interaction indicated these people were important to Kelsey. Who were they?

"Hey Jordon, how about helping us with the cooking? We need some muscle," Roger, who Jordon had learned worked in the lab, asked.

"Sure." Jordon knew nothing about cooking a low country boil but it was nice to be asked and included. Plus it kept his wandering mind off Kelsey.

At around twelve-thirty he, along with half a dozen people, helped pour buckets of corn, new potatoes, onions and shrimp over newspaper-covered tables. There were plenty of paper towel rolls available and everyone took their places at the picnic tables and dug in. With his job done, he looked for Kelsey. She was sandwiched between Josh and some other guy Jordon hadn't seen before.

One of the nurses from the E.R. called to him and moved down enough that he could join her table. The food was excellent and the conversation lively. He was glad he'd attended.

Before the first table could finish their meal and leave, the CEO stood and said through a bullhorn, "I'm glad you all could make it today. I'd like to say thanks to the picnic committee headed by Kelsey Davis for this fine event."

Kelsey had said nothing about being in charge. She'd implied she was only helping.

The CEO continued, "The games are about to begin. Please don't forget to go by and check out the silent cake auction. As an added bonus you get to share the cake with the cook. And the money goes to a good cause."

Jordon spent the next half hour making a circle around the area to see what was happening. There was apple bobbing, bingo and three-legged racing through the sand that brought smiles and laughter from everyone. A beach volleyball game was beginning when he walked up.

One of the nurses from the geriatric unit called his name and waved him over. "Come on, Jordon, we need another player."

"Sure." He took his place on her side of the net. He'd played some volleyball in the early years of high school and had been pretty good at it but his skills were rusty. What he might lack in ability he more than made up with height. Two volleys later he was able to return the ball over the net for a point, which built his confidence.

"Okay, we need this point," one of his teammates said, when it came time for him to serve.

He didn't know about getting a point, he just wanted to get the ball over the net without embarrassing himself. He gave the ball a solid hit and it did as he'd hoped. It was volleyed back. The other guy on his team returned it for a point. Jordon served again.

The number of spectators around the sandy court grew. Those in the crowd took sides and cheered for their team. This was the type of team sport experience he had missed later in high school. He'd been far too busy being angry at his mother. During the year he'd spent in military school he'd not qualified to play on any teams because he'd not attended long enough. He rather liked feeling a part of a unit, something he'd not had since his parents' divorce.

His serve soon came around again. The game was tied. He was in motion to take a swing when he noticed Kelsey standing on the edge of the field near where the pole to the net had been pushed into the ground. She had a slight smile on her face. His hand stopped in midmotion. He sucked in a breath. His gaze found hers. He remembered her all too well now. He'd seen that expression on her face before. That sweet I-only-have-eyes-for-you look.

His male pride made him want to show off. He couldn't recall purposely trying to prove his manhood through a sport ever before. Bringing his hand back, he gave the ball a hard lick. After a couple of volleys, his team earned the needed point.

"Game point, everyone," the nurse who'd invited him to play yelled. She looked at him. "Jordon, this is it."

"Thanks. No pressure."

He didn't dare look at Kelsey. He was too afraid he'd mess the serve up. Flipping the ball into the air, he punched it across the net. His male teammate tipped the returned volley back, it was returned again, and this time the nurse barely got it back over the net. It was then hit high and toward him. He had to run to get under the ball. With arms stretched out and hands fisted, he dove across the sand and popped the ball up. It just cleared the net. The other team was unable to reach the ball.

The crowd went wild. When he was on his feet again the nurse jumped into his arms, wrapping her arms around his neck. His other teammates patted him on the back.

His gaze met Kelsey's. She smiled at him and suddenly he felt like a conquering hero.

Why did her praise of all the people there have that effect on him?

Just as quickly, she turned and grabbed the arm of the man standing next to her and disappeared into the crowd. The heady feeling imploded like a building being demolished, leaving nothing but disgusted rubble.

He'd found a cold bottle of water and was coming out of the restroom after cleaning up when he heard the announcement for the water-balloon fight. He strolled over to the area of pavement where it was being held. By the time he made it to the designated area on the pavement, people surrounded it.

"Okay," Kelsey said into a bullhorn. "Teens, I want you to line up on either side of the line. Last man standing wins a cell phone. Everyone on your mark, get set, go."

Wiggly, wobbly water balloons began to fly through the air, splashing as they hit their targets. Others burst on contact with the ground and splattered the observers nearby. The kids ran from the line and back to one of the coolers he and Kelsey had loaded that morning. The crowd cheered as the number of balloon diminished. Kelsey ran up and down one side of the game field cheering the teens on and reminding them to aim for the body only. One misplaced balloon caught her on the shoulder, wetting her down one side. She laughed and kept moving.

Jordon had to give Kelsey credit. She was a dynamo. Everyone, including those surly teenagers, was having a good time.

A few minutes later the last of the balloons were gone and two dry teens still remained in the game.

Kelsey stepped out into the center of the area as if she was stepping into a boxing ring. "Well, it looks like we have a tie. Hey, Jack, could you bring that smaller cooler out here?" she called through the bullhorn. A guy walked out with a round drink cooler.

With slow, dramatic movements, Kelsey opened the screw top. The entire crowd quieted and stilled as she gently tipped over the cooler while holding the top over whatever was inside. Laying the cooler on the ground, she pulled the top away and a couple of huge water balloons rolled out like blobs of jelly.

The crowd released a universal sound of amazement.

Picking up the bullhorn again, she said, "May the best man win," then backed away.

The two teens circled the balloons before one grabbed one of the fat blobs and the other did the same with the other. Soon they were struggling to pick up their unwieldy balloons. By using their bodies, they finally managed to control the balloons enough to work them into their arms without breaking them. The crowd enjoyed the scene. Jordon was no different. One contestant became the aggressor and stalked the other then lobbed his balloon at the other. The teen sidestepped the wiggly mass and heaved the last balloon at the other teen. He moved and it hit Jordon dead center in the chest.

The water was ice cold. He sucked in a breath as his knit shirt stuck to his skin. The spectators erupted in glee but the only person Jordon could see was Kelsey, doubled over in laughter. When she stood she brought the bullhorn to her mouth. "Well, we have our winner. Dr. King, welcome to Golden Shores Hospital."

He bowed his head in her direction and she grinned. What would it be like to kiss that grin off her face and make her smile for him only? He wasn't so cold anymore.

Then she said, "Now, everyone head over to the tent for some ice cream."

The crowd shifted away. Jordon stepped through them on his way to Kelsey. She was busy picking up balloon remnants from the ground.

"You enjoyed that, didn't you?" he said, pulling his sticking shirt away from his body.

Kelsey continued what she was doing. "I did."

"Did you plan it?"

She stood, indignation written all over her face. "I did not. I couldn't have planned something so well."

Kelsey went back to what she was doing.

"Can't you leave those?" he asked, despite the beautiful view of her behind he was being given, her shorts tight across it. She had a fine derrière.

"No. They'll hurt the wildlife. I had to promise to pick it all up right away to get permission from the park service to have the balloon fight in the first place."

Where was the rest of the committee? Why wasn't someone helping her? He leaned down and started picking up broken balloon.

She stood. "You don't have to do that."

"Look at this mess. I think you can use the help."

"Your mother must have raised you right," she commented, and went back to work.

His hand faltered before he picked up the next piece of rubber. He'd never thought about that. His mother had had some positive influence in his life. All he'd remembered for years was how she had hurt his father and destroyed Jordon's trust.

Kelsey tossed the last of the broken balloons in the trash and picked up one of the coolers. He grabbed the other two empty ones. They walked to his SUV and Jordon packed the ice chests.

"How about sharing some ice cream with me?" he asked.

"I really need to check on the band." She turned toward where a group of men and a woman were setting up equipment.

His hand circled her upper arm, stopping her. She glanced at where his hand rested. He released her.

"Come on, Kelsey. You've been at it all day. Take a minute for yourself. Plus I took a balloon in your game."

"Is that an order, Doctor?"

"I would like for it not to be but if I have to make it one, I will."

She gave a resigned sigh and said, "Okay. Let me check on the band and I'll meet you over there."

"Fair enough."

Jordon circled the cake table on his way to the ice-cream tent. He needed to place a bid and help out the cause. There were a number of beautiful cakes. Beside each one lay a small card with the name of the baker and a place where a bid could be written. Looking over the offerings, he saw the cake that had sagged to one side and had a crack in it was Kelsey's. He pick up her card. The card was filled with bids.

Jordon studied the cake. They certainly weren't bidding on its merits. He looked at the card again. Kelsey didn't need his sympathy and he didn't need to be tempted by her or her cake. He was already giving her more attention that he should. Moving on, he placed his name on a couple of cards and headed to where horseshoes were being thrown.

Kelsey finished reassuring the band leader she would be around if needed and walked to where the ice cream was being served.

She had to give Jordon credit for being a good sport. For a man with his attitude toward her he seemed to take the fact in stride that her game had literally blown up on him. He'd been amazing during the volleyball game. She hadn't been able to keep her eyes off him. More than that, he'd graciously helped her pick up balloon fragments while everyone else had been having ice cream. Maybe there was still some of that guy in him that she'd had such a crush on so many years ago.

He was waiting for her when she walked up to the ice-cream line. They each got two scoops. She hadn't planned to spend any personal time with him but he hadn't given her much choice. Kelsey was searching for a place to sit when she saw her sister, China, waving her over.

"Come and sit with us," China called.

Older by two years, China had been Kelsey's best friend and protector when she'd been at home. They had grown apart after Kelsey had moved out but were making an effort to mend that gap. Kelsey had missed her sister and was glad to have her back in her life. Leaving China would be her one regret in leaving Golden Shores. Kelsey would miss her more than she wanted to admit.

Under normal circumstances she would be tickled to spend time with China and her new husband, Payton. But she worried that China might recognize Jordon. It had been too nice a day for it to be ruined by talk of Chad or, worse, their parents. Resigned, Kelsey smiled and headed her way. She was aware of Jordon following. Too aware.

The picnic table where China sat was crowded. She scooted closer to her husband and Kelsey took the spot next to her, leaving Jordon to squeeze in. His thigh brushed hers as he slipped into place. When she didn't immediately introduce him, Jordon leaned forward and looked down the table at China.

Did he know her? Somehow it would hurt if he recognized China but hadn't remembered her.

"Hi, I'm Jordon King. I work with Kelsey."

She guessed not.

China smiled at him but gave no indication that she knew him. Instead, she gave Kelsey a questioning look, as if to ask if this was her new boyfriend.

Kelsey shook her head. No one important.

"I'm China, and this is my husband, Payton." She smiled at him in complete bliss then she looked back at Jordon. "I'm Kelsey's sister."

Jordon nodded. "Nice to meet you both." His tone took on a knowing sound.

Payton asked, "So, are you new to the hospital?"

"I am. I've only been here a couple of weeks."

Kelsey was glad Payton took over the conversation so that Jordon didn't have a chance to bring up Chad. She and China had only really reconnected in the last few months. They had agreed not to discuss her parents or Chad.

"So, how do you find living in Golden Shores?" Payton asked.

Kelsey shifted. Jordon glanced at her and then said, "I'm finding it a great place to live. Stuff like this today isn't the norm around DC."

Payton grinned. "I know what you mean. I moved down here from Chicago about six months ago."

When the conversation lagged Kelsey asked, "So, China, did you bring a cake for the contest?"

"I did. A sour cream pound cake." She smiled lovingly at her husband. "It's Payton's favorite."

Would she ever find a relationship like theirs? Maybe when she got out of Golden Shores there would be someone for her who would put that sparkle in her eyes.

"Payton has placed a bid so high that I don't think anyone will match it," China said. "Did you bring one?"

"I did, but it doesn't look like much. That was always your department." Kelsey scooted back. "It's almost time for the auction to be over. I'd better go check on things."

There was no graceful way to get out from between China and Jordon without placing her hands on their shoulders for support. There was a marked difference between China's thin, petite one and Jordon's large, muscular shoulder.

"I'm tired so we won't be staying for the dance," China said.

"Are you feeling okay?" Kelsey looked down at her with concern.

"Never better. I was going to tell you Tuesday when we have lunch but I can't wait."

Payton slipped his arm around China's waist and smiled up at Kelsey.

"I'm pregnant," China announced.

Kelsey squealed and leaned over to hug her. "That's wonderful."

When she tipped forward too far, strong hands steadied her until she was on her feet again. Heat rose to her face and she glanced away from China to find her face entirely too close to Jordon's. "Thanks," she murmured.

"Now maybe you'll rethink moving to Atlanta. I want your niece or nephew to know you," China said softly, for Kelsey's ear only. The pleading tone pulled at Kelsey's heart. Still, she couldn't give up her dream.

"They'll know me. You can come visit often," Kelsey whispered.

Her name was called and she waved at the man across the park.

"Go on," China said. "I'll see you Tuesday. We'll talk more then."

Leaving them behind, she headed to see what Walter wanted. A twinge of worry ran through her. Surely Jordon wouldn't get into a personal discussion with her sister and Payton about their shared past.

An hour later Kelsey was standing behind the table where her cake sat along with all the other people who had baked one. All the final bids had been made and now the winners were being announced. Despite the awful mess her cake was, she'd had a full bid sheet when she'd last checked. Obviously there was compassion in the world. From what she could tell, the cake auction would make a nice sum of money for the children's ward redecoration.

"Alice Reynolds's cake was won by Mark Dobson.

Come up and claim your cake and the baker. All right, the next cake was made by Nancy Mitchell. And the winner of that cake is Jordon King."

Kelsey's head jerked round. The smiling Nancy from the business office. Her unofficial date competitor. Nancy was going to be sharing her cake with Jordon. Why should Kelsey care? She'd seen more of him today than she'd wanted to. Still, it bothered her on a level she didn't understand. Had he even bid on hers?

"Well…" She leaned over and said to Molly, "I guess you just lost your bet."

"Winning her cake doesn't constitute a date. Being asked out does," she whispered back.

Two cakes later it was her turn.

"And the winner of Kelsey's cake is Reid Johnson."

Reid worked in the E.R. and was a nice enough guy. He'd asked her out a number of times but she just wasn't interested. She smiled, picked up her cake and went to meet Reid. He took the cake from her and led her over to a nearby table. To her dismay, it was close to where Jordon sat with Nancy.

"Uh, wouldn't you rather sit in the shade?" she asked.

"No, this is fine," Reid said, putting the cake down.

"Then I'll get us some forks and plates and something to cut with."

"Hey, would you mind getting us some too?" Jordon called.

She couldn't say that she did mind or why, so she nodded. "Sure." The man was starting to get under her skin.

As she returned with the plates and utensils, a loud burst of laughter came from Jordon and Nancy's direction. Kelsey walked to their table and placed the things Jordon had requested on it.

"Thanks, Kelsey," Jordon said as he picked up the plastic knife, giving her no more attention.

Nancy offered a coy smile as if she thought she'd won the prize. Kelsey had never had anything against Nancy but apparently she saw Kelsey as a rival, which certainly was not the case. Kelsey had no designs on Jordon.

"You guys enjoy!" she said as brightly as she could, and went back to where Reid waited. She and Reid shared a slice of her cake while he told her a joke. Kelsey laughed. She looked up to find Jordon glaring at her. Turning her shoulder to him, she continued her conversation with Reid, which included more humor.

The sun was beginning to set when the band struck up a tune. The people still there drifted toward the dance area in front of the makeshift stage. Kelsey left Reid with the rest of her cake and went to check on an issue in the food tent. For the next couple of hours she only saw Jordon from a distance. Each time she did Nancy was beside him, even to the point of hanging on his arm. It was no big deal. Nancy could have him. So why did she keep looking around to see where they were?

Kelsey danced a few dances but spent most of the last minutes of daylight cleaning and packing up. As soon as the dance was over she would be on her way home to bed. Exhausted didn't even describe how tired she felt. She was circling the floor, picking up forgotten drink cups, when a finger tapped her shoulder.

"I wouldn't be a gentleman if I didn't dance with the one that brung me," said a voice she knew far too well after such a short period of time.

"That's not necessary and I think you distorted the saying some."

"I know, but that's beside the point. Instead of correcting me, how about being friendly enough to accept my offer to dance?" He extended his hand.

She didn't want to appear mean by not agreeing, but instead of taking his hand she walked onto the dance floor and waited. When he reached her his hand came to rest snugly on her waist, giving her the feeling of being imprisoned and protected at the same time. She placed her hands on his shoulders. Her fingertips traced the corded muscle beneath them.

She met Jordon's gaze. "You know, I can find a way home if you want to leave with Nancy."

"Jealous?" he asked with a grin.

Kelsey stopped moving. "I am not. You have to care to be jealous. I was just trying to be nice."

One of his arms slipped further around her back and pulled her closer but not so close that they touched.

"Hush and let's enjoy the dance. I brought you, I'll be taking you home," he murmured, as he slowly led her around the floor.

Being in Jordon's arms made her feel jittery, unsure and out of sorts. She rarely felt any of these and never in a combination. She'd worked too hard and for too long to lose control over her emotions. She didn't like them escaping.

They swayed to the music until the last note. She was walking away from Jordon when the bandleader called for the last dance. Nancy passed her, headed in the direction Kelsey had come from.

A half an hour later, true to his word, Kelsey was sitting beside Jordon as he pulled his vehicle out of the parking lot. "That was a lot of fun," he said, with a contented tone in his voice.

"Yeah, they always are. Picnics on the beach are one of the few things I'm going to miss about this place."

He quickly glanced at her. "Miss?"

"I'm hoping to get a job in Atlanta. I'm expecting a call to set up an interview any day."

"That's news."

"I've not told many people. I'd like you to keep it to yourself," she said, as she leaned her head against the doorframe and closed her eyes.

Kelsey eyelids opened when Jordon turned the motor off. She hadn't planned to sleep.

"You're exhausted. Why don't you go on in and I'll unload?"

"No, I'll help."

He shrugged. "I was just trying to be nice." He then went around to the back of the SUV and started pulling out the coolers. She unlocked the door to the house and flipped lights on as she walked into the kitchen. Jordon followed, setting the coolers on the floor.

Her phone buzzed against her hip. Pulling it out, she answered it. "Hey, Paul. No problem. I'm just getting home."

"I forgot to ask you if you would be willing to remain on the committee for the picnic next year?"

"I don't know. Can I give you an answer closer to the time?"

"Sure. See you soon."

"Bye." She placed the phone on the counter.

Jordon stood with his arms across his chest and a hip against the cabinet.

She propped fisted hands on her hips. "Why're you always glaring at me?"

"Glaring?"

"Yeah. Glaring. Like this." She hunched her shoulders slightly, thrust her chin out, squinted and looked pointedly at him. "Glaring. What have I done to you?"

"Maybe I'm just trying to figure you out. Like why you

have that wild hair. Why nothing is peaceful when you are around. Why men are always hanging around you."

She straightened and narrowed her eyes. "Why should it matter to you why men hang around me?"

"It doesn't."

"Then why mention it?"

"Because…aw, hell…" Jordon grabbed her and brought his mouth down to hers. It wasn't a tender kiss but one born of frustration. The entire day he'd thought of kissing her. Had watched her smile at all the men. Now it was his time to have her complete attention. Force her to really notice him.

She made a startled sound of surprise. Her mouth opened and he took advantage of the opportunity to dip into the warm cavern before backing off and nipping questioningly at her lips. They were as sweet as he'd imagined they might be.

Kelsey's hands gripped his waist as she stepped toward him.

Jordon released her as suddenly as he'd taken her. He had to remember that caring could turn and bite you. Still, he wanted her. Didn't want to want her. Wished she'd want him.

He wouldn't give Kelsey the power to hurt him like his ex-girlfriend had. Wouldn't become one of the herd of men who fell under her seductive power. His ex had woven such a perfect picture that he hadn't been able to see the truth about her and what she'd been doing until it had been far too late. Not again. That was a chance he refused to take. Kelsey could easily hurt him the same way. He would keep her at arm's length. After all, she was leaving soon.

Kelsey rocked back. His hands remained on her until she steadied then he let go. Her eyes were filled with questions.

"Don't ask me why," he growled, and stalked out.

CHAPTER FOUR

KELSEY WASN'T SURE what had just happened. Had she been kissed or punished? What wasn't she supposed to ask about? The kiss or why he'd quit?

Since she'd been fourteen boys had been attracted to her. She'd dated a lot but had never had a serious relationship. Sure, she'd had a couple of boyfriends but she'd never considered marrying them. They had been local guys. Her future plans hadn't included staying in Golden Shores. Marrying a local would have held her here. She was having nothing of that.

Until Jordon's kiss she would have said he scarcely tolerated her. He'd been helpful today but still he seemed to spend more time than not giving her disapproving looks. What had she ever done to him?

It was more like what he'd done to her. She had been the girl with the broken heart when he'd left without even saying goodbye. As irrational as she'd felt as a young girl, she'd been crushed. She'd worn the plastic ring every day for over a year and cried each night for half that time. If she wasn't careful the man would do the same thing to her again. But this time it would be her leaving with the broken heart. Because she was leaving.

As pretty as Saturday had been for the picnic, by Monday the wind had increased and the weather report sounded more ominous. As Kelsey entered the hospital a gust lifted her skirt and she pushed it back into place. She arrived at her office and unlocked it.

Molly had left early that morning for a meeting in Jackson. Kelsey fussed about her returning with the tropical depression coming in. Molly assured her that she'd be fine. The weatherman reported the worst of the storm was headed to the west of them but the area would get massive amounts of wind and rain. Golden Shores wasn't required to evacuate but, still, the weatherman recommended people stay put for twenty-four hours. Even that would bring in a boatload of patients.

Clicking on her computer, Kelsey scanned her emails and saw one she had been expecting glowing brightly. The hospital was on alert, which meant she wouldn't be going home tonight. Worse than that there was no dodging Jordon.

As the day progressed the wind increased to the point that windows rattled. The sky darkened enough that the security lights in the parking lot came on. By the time Kelsey returned to her car to claim the small bag she'd packed with extra toiletries and clothes, the air had taken on a heavy feel.

In the middle of the afternoon the rain began to fall. At every nursing station the hurricane was the topic of conversation and TVs were set to the weather channel. Minutes before four o'clock her cell phone rang. It was Jim, letting her know it was time for their team to meet in the lobby. She hurried to her office and changed from her skirt and frilly blouse into her knit shirt with the hospital staff logo, jeans and tennis shoes.

Her group was already busy setting up behind one of the support walls in the lobby for protection if the storm worsened. The area was constructed of tall all-glass windows but it was the largest area available. Since the brunt of the storm wasn't coming their direction it was being used as the emergency room overflow.

"Hey, Josh, are we expecting patients right away?" she asked.

"Not right this sec. We're the first group backing up the ER. There's been an accident on the highway and the ER is covered with incoming. We're to handle any minor injuries here."

"Okay. I'll be ready." She went in search of the paperwork she would need to fill out on each patient. Jim handed her a clipboard that he'd just pulled out of their supply box. Staff members worked setting up portable tables for patients and rearranging the lobby into a make-shift waiting area.

With clipboard in hand, Kelsey walked over to look out one of the windows. The rain pounded against the glass. She could no longer see the highway in front of the building.

"I forgot how fearsome a Gulf storm can be."

Her pulse quickened. *Jordon.*

"Yes, they are something. I've ridden out so many that I don't get too upset about them anymore."

"About the other night…"

She turned to face him. "Look, I'm not starting anything with you, Jordon. I'm hoping to move soon. I don't need the headache."

"I want to apologize for walking out like I did. I'm not looking for a relationship either."

An elderly couple coming up the walk drew her attention away from Jordon's statement. They were huddled against the sideways rain with no umbrella in sight. One of them was obviously assisting the other.

Jordon hurried to the door and she was right behind

him. He had the door open and almost pulled the couple into the building when Kelsey reached them. The woman was bleeding.

"Kelsey, get a couple of blankets," Jordon said.

As she ran to the rolling cart where the blankets were stacked, she passed Josh. "We have a patient."

"I'm on my way."

By the time she returned, Jordon had the woman in a chair. He and Josh worked to stop the bleeding from a laceration to her head. Kelsey left a blanket with Josh and went to the forlorn-looking man sitting in the waiting area.

She sank into the chair next to him.

"Hi, I'm Kelsey. How about me helping you take off your coat and let's put this dry blanket over your shoulders."

"Okay," the man murmured, his teeth chattering.

She went through the slow process of helping to remove his coat. With that done, she pulled the blanket over his back.

"Why don't you tell me what happened?" Kelsey had learned from past experience that patients or their caregivers wanted to talk first. After they had that chance she didn't have any problem getting answers to her official questions.

"I told her, my Bernice, not to go out and get that last potted plant. The wind and rain were getting too strong. But she didn't listen. She loves those blasted plants too much." He looked with such love and concern at the woman who Jordon was preparing to stitch up.

What would that kind of love feel like?

"The hanging basket swung and hit her in the head. Blood went everywhere and she felt dizzy. I knew it was bad, so we had no choice but to come here."

Kelsey patted his age-spotted hand. "You did the right

thing. Dr. King will take care of your wife." She was confident she was telling him the truth. Even though she hadn't known Jordon that long, he was a good doctor. She could say that with complete confidence.

"If it's okay with you, I'd like to get some information now." Kelsey picked up her clipboard and pen from the nearby chair where she'd left it.

The man nodded and sat a little straighter.

For the next few minutes Kelsey took down the woman's personal information. As she finished, Jordon joined them.

"Mr. Lingerfelt?"

The man nodded.

"Your wife is going to be just fine. I've had to put in a few stitches but she'll be as pretty as ever."

Mr. Lingerfelt lifted his lips in a tired smile.

"I'd like to admit her so we can make sure she doesn't have a concussion. You two don't need to be out in this weather anyway. You'll be a lot safer here. We don't have any stylish clothes for you to change into but we do have some dry ones. How does that sound?"

"I wasn't looking forward to driving in that." He glanced toward the window.

Jordon looked that direction too. "I don't blame you."

"Kelsey, would you see Mr. Lingerfelt back to where Mrs. Lingerfelt is?"

"Sure." Kelsey waited for the man to rise. Together they walked to the treatment area.

"Oh, Bernice, honey," Mr. Lingerfelt said as he approached his wife.

"I'm fine, Walter. You can say I told you so later. The nice doctor said he wants me to stay tonight. He'll let you stay too."

"I know." Mr. Lingerfelt took his wife's hand and held it.

"We'll pretend we're camping like we did on our honeymoon," Mrs. Lingerfelt said with a weak grin.

Kelsey couldn't help but smile. The image of these two spending their honeymoon in a tent in the woods gave her a warm feeling.

One of the nurses from the second floor entered the area, pushing a wheelchair.

"This nurse will be taking you to your room," Kelsey said.

"Will you be seeing that nice Dr. King?"

Kelsey nodded. Jordon *was* nice. She hadn't given him much of a chance but he'd managed anyway. "Yes."

"Tell him I said not to give up on that girl."

What girl? Did Jordon have someone in town he was interested in already? She smiled and said, "I'll tell him."

By the time she returned to the lobby, Jordon was with another patient. Hours raced by as they cared for a patient with a cut to the hand he'd received trying to keep a piece of tin from flying into another person. A broken arm had come next, followed by another patient who'd had a foreign object in her eye.

It was after nine p.m. before they got a break.

"Let's get a sandwich and a drink, and sit while we can," Jordon said. The cafeteria staff had set up a table with food toward the back of the lobby.

Jim and Josh were already moving in that direction.

"I'm coming. I have one more thing that needs to be done."

"Let it wait. You look like you could use a rest. I'd bet that, like me, you haven't eaten since lunch."

She didn't like admitting it but he was right. "You go on. I'll be right behind you."

"No, I'm going to wait because I think you'll get sidetracked doing something for someone if I don't."

Kelsey huffed and put down the clipboard and pen. "Satisfied?" She looked around. They were relatively alone. She placed her hands on her hips. "For someone who wants nothing to do with me you sure like to tell me what to do."

Something flared in his eyes. "I didn't say that I didn't want to have anything to do with you. I said I don't want a relationship."

"What does that mean?"

He took a step closer. "It means I want to kiss you but I have no intention of marrying you."

"So I'm good enough to have sex with but not to take home to your mother?"

"I don't care what my mother thinks."

That sounded a little harsh. What was the deal with his mother?

"Hey, you two had better come on and get something to eat before the next patient shows up," Josh called.

Kelsey moved towards the back, picked out a premade sandwich and pulled a canned drink out of the bucket filled with ice. There weren't enough chairs for everyone so she slid down the wall with a sigh and sat on the floor. To her dismay, Jordon joined her.

"You could have taken the last chair," she said.

"I would have felt bad about doing that while you sat on the floor."

"Go on and take the chair. I don't mind sitting here. I'm comfortable."

"If I didn't know better, I'd think you were trying to get rid of me."

If the truth be known, she was. "Suit yourself." She took a bite out of her sandwich.

Jordon settled in beside her but not within touching distance. They ate in silence. He finished before she did and leaned back and closed his eyes. A few minutes went by. Was he asleep?

"You know, you're going to miss all this kind of excitement if you leave town."

She looked at him. His eyes were still closed. The slump of his shoulders said he was tired as she was, and they still had the rest of the night to get through. The weather would get worse before it got better.

"I don't think I'll miss this or anything else for that matter."

"Ooh, that has an unforgiving sound to it. A slam on me."

"I don't know you well enough to miss you. I'm just ready to get out of Golden Shores."

"So tell me about this new job." He still hadn't opened his eyes.

"Shhh, my boss doesn't know I'm looking. I don't want him to find out some way other than from me telling him."

He opened one eye. "Sorry." He went on, "I can't imagine someone as well liked as you wanting to leave."

"So I guess since you're here you weren't well liked in Washington."

"I was liked. I just made some bad decisions. Stood behind the wrong people."

"How's that?"

"I really would rather not talk about it. There were issues."

"Well, I have some issues about being here."

"Like what?"

"Like I've been trying to get out of Golden Shores since I was eighteen. Now's my chance." Kelsey picked up her sandwich wrapper and drink can. Pushing against the wall, she stood. She looked down at him pointedly. "This place holds some bad memories for me."

She started to walk away then stopped. "By the way," she threw over her shoulder, "I forgot to give you Mrs. Lingerfelt's message. She said for you not to give up on that girl."

Kelsey didn't ask what it meant or even who the girl was. It was none of her business. Still, she wanted to know more than she was willing to admit.

Jordon didn't doubt that there were some unhappy memories for Kelsey in Golden Shores. How would there not be with her brother disappearing? It hadn't always been happy times for him in Golden Shores either but the good memories far outshone the bad. Had what had happened with Chad affected her that much or was there something more?

He didn't have time during the night to ask her. If he had he wasn't sure that she would have answered him. They were busy most of the time with minor injuries. At three thirty-five the electricity blinked off. It took a few minutes for the back-up generators to kick in and the lights flickered on again.

Around six a.m. Jordon saw Kelsey take out her phone. She stayed on the line for a few seconds then slipped the phone back into her pocket. He returned to filling out paperwork on his most recent patient. Some time later he noticed her with her phone out again. Was she worried about her parents? Sister?

Jim give him the word that the worst was over. They could all go home their last patient was taken care of. Kelsey was standing in a nearby corner with the phone to her ear when he walked up to give her the news. As he approached he noticed her brows were drawn together and she was pacing. Kelsey glanced at him. Her eyes were heavy with moisture on the verge of falling.

"What's wrong?" His tone demanded an answer.

"I can't find Molly," she blurted out, close to a sob.

"Molly?"

"My roommate. She works here."

"Isn't she on call, like the rest of us? Is she here in the hospital?"

As if she'd run out of patience she said, "No. She was out of town for a meeting. She should've been back but she's not answering her phone. I'm worried something has happened."

"So where should she be?"

"At home."

"Come on. I'll drive."

"I can go myself."

"I have no doubt that you can but I think you'll get there much faster in my SUV. I was just in the E.R. and one of the ambulance drivers said that the roads are a mess with debris and flooding. So do you want to take a chance in your low-to-the-ground car or—?"

"Let's go." She started toward the employees' entrance, pulling her cell from her pocket at the same time.

The storm still blew rain crosswise as they ran for his SUV. Kelsey hadn't even attempted to use an umbrella. It would have been a complete waste of time against the torrent. During one gust Jordon grabbed her arm to help steady her. He took her hand and held it until they reached the SUV. After climbing in they both huffed with the exertion it took to move around in the awful weather. They sat for a second or two before Jordon reached into the backseat and pulled a towel forward.

"Hardy sits on it when he rides. I don't think he'll mind if we use it under the circumstances."

That gained him a half smile before Kelsey took a corner and started wiping water from her face. He used the opposite corner and did the same. She let the towel drop and struggled to pull her phone from her hip pocket. He didn't miss the way her wet T-shirt molded to her breasts. Despite his concern over her worry for her friend, he still had the hots for her. Maybe he didn't want a relationship, but he sure wanted her. It might be short as she was planning to leave town, but it would sure be sweet while it lasted.

Kelsey put the phone to her ear as he cranked the SUV. "Still nothing?"

Kelsey shook her head and lowered the phone with a look of disappointment and escalating fear.

"Okay. Let's go find her. I bet she's in bed and can't hear her phone over the wind."

He maneuvered around limbs that littered the parking lot and one palm listed badly to the left near the picnic area. Main Street was deserted but he stayed toward the middle of the road to avoid the deep pockets of water. The drains were overflowing in their efforts to handle the runoff. It was slow going. Traffic lights were out and the few cars he passed were driving far too fast for the conditions.

One car threw enough water over them to cover the windshield. He cursed low as he had to strain to see. He glanced at Kelsey. She leaned forward, peering through the glass with both hands clamped to the dash. Everything about her demeanor screamed she was terrified.

"She's going to be fine."

"You can't know that," she snapped.

"No, I can't."

"I'm sorry. I'm just so scared."

He reached over and took one of her hands and squeezed it before letting it go.

As he attempted to turn right into their road he slowed to a stop. A beach oak had fallen across the road.

"I don't think I can drive across it. I'm going to see about moving some limbs so maybe we can get around it." Jordon climbed out of the SUV and was soaked completely before he reached the tree. Kelsey was there beside him to help as he picked up the second limb.

"Get back in the SUV," he yelled.

"It'll go faster with two of us working."

They pulled branches out of the way and went back for more. After moving as much as they could without a chainsaw Jordon called, "I think I can get around now."

If there had been any dry clothes on them before, there weren't now. He turned the heat on high then started slowing rolling over a large branch they hadn't been able to move. The leafy top of the tree hindered his sight. Seconds later they were on their way again down the dark road. In one area a power pole had snapped and the line lay on the ground. There was barely enough space for him to skirt it.

Kelsey hissed and jumped in his direction as sparks shot in the air when the line bounced against the pavement. He laid a hand on her back in reassurance before returning his attention back to the downed line, making sure not to touch it.

As they passed her parents' house, he glanced at it and saw she was looking too. "You want to stop and check on them?"

"No. I've already talked to China. They're fine."

Jordon said no more and continued to drive at a slow and steady pace. He worked to see through the gloom ahead. He ached between his shoulder blades. The sky was growing lighter behind them but wasn't making much headway against the heavy cloud cover and rain. He remained in the center of the road to miss the water gushing along either side. With a swift turn of the wheel he dodged a large limb in the road. They were approaching his house when Kelsey gasped. He looked further ahead. A huge oak tree lay on the roof of the back half of her bungalow.

"Molly's car is there." She pointed. He could make out a small red car sitting in the drive close to the house.

He made a quick turn into his drive.

Kelsey looked at him in shock and demanded, "What're you doing?"

"I'm going to get Hardy. You stay here." Jordon climbed out, not waiting for her to answer. He ran for the house, opened the door and Hardy almost knocked him over in his zest to go out.

"Let's go, boy."

He returned to the SUV to find Kelsey gone. Why wasn't he surprised? She'd better not have gone and done something impulsive and gotten herself hurt. He opened the door of the SUV for Hardy and they both jumped in. Seconds later, Jordon pulled into Kelsey's drive. Letting Hardy out, he grabbed his emergency medical bag from the rear floorboard and a flashlight out of the glove compartment. He and the dog ran for the open door of the house. The faint sound of Kelsey's voice calling Molly's name came from deep inside the dark house.

"Kelsey!" he yelled. "For heaven's sake, stay put. The whole place may come down on your head."

He saw a flash of light off to the right and under where the tree had hit. His heart caught in his throat.

"Over here, Jordon," she called.

He moved toward the dim light. "Did you find her?"

"No." The sound was almost a sob.

Hardy rushed past him and was now barking somewhere ahead to Jordon's left.

"Good boy. I'll be right there." Jordon headed toward Kelsey.

When he reached her she was moving her cell phone flashlight in a frantic motion backward and forward among the limbs of the tree in the area of what he guessed had been a bedroom.

"I can't find her," Kelsey said, her voice filled with panic.

Hardy continued to bark, the sound becoming more urgent.

"Hardy has found her." Jordon was afraid to say any more. "Follow me and do exactly as I tell you." He looked at her. "Do you understand?"

She nodded. Maybe her fear would keep her in check. As they moved further down what had once been a hallway and under the tree, she grabbed on to the back of his shirt and let him be the guide. Jordon had no idea what to expect but he didn't want Kelsey to see her friend first. He helped Kelsey climb over a rain-slick branch and under another until they managed to squeeze between limbs to where Hardy stood barking.

Jordon made sure to keep his body between Kelsey and the sight ahead of him. Molly was trapped under a branch. All he could see were her legs.

He turned and Kelsey let go of his shirt. Cupping her shoulders and looking at her intently, Jordon said, "Kelsey, Hardy has found her. Don't fall apart on me. I'm going to need your help."

She stuck out her chest as if she was preparing to fight. "I'm not going to fall apart," she said in a strong, defiant voice.

"Good. Now, hold the light. I have to crawl under and get her vitals. Hardy, hush. Sit."

The dog obeyed.

He didn't need to waste any more time. How long had Molly been lying under this tree? Placing his bag on the floor, he went down on his knees. He felt along Molly's body. At least she was wearing jeans. That would have helped prevent some injuries. Finally he found her neck. With great relief he located a pulse but it was weak. "She's alive."

"Thank God."

"We've got to get her to the hospital ASAP. She isn't in good shape."

"What do I need to do?" Kelsey's voice sounded strong and sure.

She must be rattled if she was allowing him to make the decisions.

"Call 911 and have them send the wagon. Push my bag under here." Kelsey picked up his bag from where he'd dropped it and shoved it toward the sound of his voice. She was more grateful than she could express to have Jordon there. Without him and Hardy, it would have taken her much longer to find Molly.

Punching 911, she told the dispatcher she needed an ambulance at 3564 Bay Road. The dispatcher said that because of the storm all the ambulances were out and it would be a while. She relayed the information to Jordon. His expletive mirrored her concern.

"Okay, then. We'll have to do this ourselves."

"We can't move her. We might hurt her more." She could only make out a shadowed outline of Jordon beneath the fallen tree and the shambles of the roof. Rain still fell but not as hard as earlier.

"Kelsey, take a deep breath. Molly is going to be fine."

Somehow his strong presence and reassurance made her believe him.

"Find some blankets. We need to treat for shock and keep her warm. Along with blankets we also need something flat and strong to lay her on." He said the words more in a reflective tone than in one issuing orders. "Go to my SUV. There are some straps and bungee cords there. Bring them. Also, while you are there lay the seats down. It will be a job but you're going to have to pull the back one out. We'll take her to the hospital ourselves if the ambulance doesn't make it. Can you handle all that?"

"I'll get it done."

"Good. Now get going. And, Kelsey, be careful."

She was crawling over the first limb when Jordon yelled, "Take Hardy with you."

"Hardy," she called, and the dog moved past her and through the brush. She came out from under the tree and into the living area. The brunt of the damage had been to Molly's bedroom.

Kelsey snatched the throw quilts off the chair and couch. Going through the tree again, she said when she got to Jordon and Molly. "Here are the blankets."

"Great. Do you see my hand?" His arm came out of the leaves a couple of feet in front of her.

"Yeah."

"Put them as close to my hand as you can."

Kelsey did as he said. "I'll be back in a minute with the other stuff."

"Kelsey." The sound of her name carried a warm note. "You're doing great."

Frightened beyond belief, she needed those encouraging words. She had a job to do. Jordon depended on her. Molly's life rested in their hands. Kelsey would do everything in her power not to disappoint either of them. Working her way back through the tree, she hurried outside. Hardy followed.

Using her phone's flashlight so she didn't fall, Kelsey went around to the back of the house where her surfboard was stored, hoping the tree hadn't gotten it also. It had been knocked over but, thank goodness, it was still there. Putting her surfboard under her arm, she carried it to the door and leaned it against the house. Now for Jordon's SUV. Hardy stayed with her, never more than a few paces away.

She wasn't sure why Jordon had sent the dog with her, but she liked having another breathing soul around as she worked in the dark and rain. Rushing to the SUV, she open the back door and searched with her light for the straps. They lay in a pile in the corner. *Great.* She gathered them and dropped them on the ground beside the SUV. Now all she had to do was figure out how to lay the seats flat.

Opening the passenger door, she searched for a lever to pull or a button to push. Finding a lever, Kelsey managed to fold the middle passenger seat down. She ran to the other side and did the same with the other seat. Going to the back of the SUV, she climbed inside and pushed the button on top of the rear seat, folding it over onto itself. After some frustrating moments she located the handle she needed to pull to release the rear seat. Pushing, pulling and shoving, she managed to get the large, cumbersome seat to the open door. She wasn't strong enough to lift the seat so she let it slide down the bumper to the ground. Climbing out, she pulled it away from the vehicle. She gave a brief thought to the fact it might never be the same again. But that didn't matter. Molly did.

She bundled the soaked straps and cords into her arms and headed for the house. Inside it was nice to have a moment that water wasn't running down her face. Again she worked her way back to reach Jordon and Molly.

"How's she doing?" Kelsey asked, depositing the straps in the same place she'd put the blankets. If it weren't for the low glow of the flashlight she wouldn't have had any idea that Jordon and Molly were underneath.

"She's holding her own but we need to get her out of here."

CHAPTER FIVE

"I'LL BE RIGHT BACK." Kelsey made her way to the door again. *This was going to be the tricky part.* She had to get the long surfboard between the tree branches. She kicked the fin until it broke, falling to the ground. She nudged it out of the pathway space with her foot. Molly would owe her a new surfboard when she got well. She had to get well.

Taking the strap in her hand, she pulled it across the floor. The board became hung up and she had to go to the back and straighten it before it would move further. All the time Hardy was nearby, barking encouragement. It took a while but she fought her way back to Jordon.

With a huff of exhaustion and exasperation she called, "I've got the board."

"Good girl. I need you to slide it under here and then climb under and help me get Molly on it."

Kelsey took a deep breath. Sweat and rain had long ago mixed on her face. Her jeans stuck to her. Leaves and dirt covered her hair but none of that mattered. She placed the board so that it was flat on the floor and started pushing it under the limbs until she had it straight. Sliding it along the floor, she got on her hands and knees and shoved it toward Jordon.

"That's good. Keep it coming. What is this?"

"My surfboard."

"I should have known you'd be resourceful."

His amazement and admiration fueled her tired, sore muscles. This wasn't a man who tried to control her, like her father had. Jordon had faith in her.

"Okay, that's far enough. Come on in."

She had to crawl alongside the board and then squeeze into a pocket under the tree on the opposite side of the board from Jordon. She sucked in a breath. Her hands shook. Molly lay on her back, her skin pasty white even in the dim light.

"Kelsey, now is not the time to lose it," Jordon said in a firm voice. "Look at me." She did. "Molly needs us both to hold it together. I can't help her if I'm worried about you. We've got this."

He saw them as a team. She had to do her part. Would do it.

"Tell me what you need me to do."

"We're going to need to get her on a flat surface. I'm not going to lie to you and tell you this will be easy. Molly is unconscious and we'll have to lift her weight in this small area."

The worst of the rain was being averted by part of the roof and the tree limbs. For that she was grateful.

"I'll do what I have to."

He looked her straight in the eyes. "I know you will. Okay, we need to spread the straps out at a uniform distance so they're positioned under the board."

Jordon had wasted no time preparing to move Molly. He'd already untangled the mass she'd left him. They placed the straps beside and horizontal to Molly's body. Jordon laid one end across Molly at her chest, hips and thighs.

"I hate to say this but you're going to need to move as far back as you can so that we can pull the surfboard alongside Molly. Kelsey scooted back on her knees until she was under the tree as far as she could go. Limbs poked into her head and sides.

"Okay, if you can reach the board, move it alongside Molly and over the straps, making sure the straps ends can be reached." Jordon came up on his knees with his shoulders hunched in what appeared to be an uncomfortable position for someone so large. Leaning over Molly's legs, he grasped the end of the board.

Kelsey's fingers gripped the edge of the board but she managed a better hold as Jordon's greater strength pulled it forward.

"You guide while I pull," he groaned, breathing heavily.

With him tugging, she made sure the board didn't hit Molly. They managed to get it into position with it and Molly between them. Kelsey watched the straps, making sure they remained in the correct place.

"You ready for the tough part?"

She nodded.

"Now, we've got to lift Molly onto the board. I'm going to run a hand under her shoulders. I've already put a neck brace on her but I want to keep her as steady as possible. From this position it will be difficult. I need you to see that her legs and butt get on the board at the same time. Can you do that?"

"I'll do it."

He gave her a supportive smile. "I know you will. On my count of three."

Kelsey moved to the narrowest part of the board. From her awkward position, Kelsey put both arms under Molly's thighs.

"One, two, three."

She lifted. Her muscles complained but she managed to bring Molly's legs toward her chest and up over the edge of the board. She imagined that her ache and pains were little compared to what Jordon was experiencing as he lifted the heavier part of Molly's body from that cramped angle.

Kelsey slid Molly across, then went to the end of the board and adjusted her legs so that they rested on the board. Shifting back to the side again, she moved Molly's hips until they were in the middle of the board. She looked to see how Jordon was doing. He'd gotten her upper body on the board and was now lifting her eyelids, shining a penlight into them.

"Still dilated and unresponsive," he murmured.

He didn't sound pleased.

Jordon looked at her. "Good job. Now we need to cover her with the blankets and get her strapped down."

They worked together, putting the covering over her body and placing the straps and cords across it.

"Use one of these bungee cords to hold her feet in place." he said.

Kelsey wrapped the two hooked ends together across Molly's ankles. She looked at Jordon for further instructions. His gaze met hers. She didn't miss the admiration in his eyes.

"Now comes the even tougher job. We've got to get her under this unholy mess on this unbending contraption." He pushed a leaf off his face. "Then it's out to the SUV."

"We can do it."

"That's what I like to hear. A positive attitude. I'll pull from the front and you push from the back." He thrust his bag out ahead of him then crawled past Molly's feet through the opening.

With tears falling, Kelsey cupped Molly's cheek. "Oh, Molly, I'm so sorry this happened to you." She didn't have time to say more before the board started moving. Kelsey remained on her knees and pushed. The wet surface let the straps slid along the floor, instead of bunching up and coming off. They reached the first limb and by a narrow margin were able to pull Molly beneath it. The next one would be the problem. Jordon stopped.

"I'm going to see if I can lift this limb some. See if you can find a chair or something to prop it up on. We need to get it off the floor enough that we can slide her under."

Kelsey climbed out and fought her way down what had once been the hallway to her bedroom. She dumped the clothes she'd left lying on her favorite overstuffed chair on the floor and started dragging the chair down to where Jordon and Molly waited. "Will this do?"

"Yeah that should work." Jordon said, "Turn it over on its side."

She flipped it.

"When I get this high enough, I want you to push the chair under."

He wrapped his arms around the limb and began lifting. After a groan from Jordon the tree began to move. Kelsey grabbed the limb, lifting upwards. Once it was high enough she let go and shoved the chair beneath it.

Jordon let go, releasing a huff. Standing, he rubbed his back. "We've got to get her under as fast as we can. I don't know how long the chair will hold."

Kelsey crawled beneath the tree and got behind the board. Jordon started pulling and the surfboard with Molly on it moved through the opening. Kelsey crawled under the branch when the chair made cracking noises. The next second she was jerked by her arms out from under the limb and across Jordon's prone body. A moment later the tree made a thudding noise and the leaves surrounding them shook.

She shuddered and looked up. Jordon's face was inches from hers. The warmth of his breath caressed her forehead.

"Are you okay?" The words were raspy with emotion as his hand touched her face.

"I'm fine," she managed to get out.

"Good. Let's get Molly to the hospital." Jordon moved, tipping her off him. He stood and helped her stand. With him pulling and her steering, they managed to get Molly to the kitchen door.

"I'll back the SUV as close to the door as I can get."

Jordon went out, with his head down, into the stream of rain that had started again. He was something special. That hero he'd been when she'd been a kid was fast becoming shiny again.

Molly moaned. It was the first sound she'd made since they'd started to move her.

"Mol, it's Kelsey. We're trying to get you to the hospital. You should be there soon."

Red brake lights flashed as Jordon moved the SUV into position in front of the door. Seconds later he opened the back doors to the SUV wide.

"We need to lift her head in first. Then we'll slide her the rest of the way."

"She's starting to come to."

"Then we need to get moving. She'll be in a lot of pain when she does."

Jordon lifted the front end of the surfboard and Kelsey the back as they eased out the narrow door of the house. Outside, Jordon placed his end of the board in the SUV. No longer able to carry her friend, Kelsey placed her end on the ground.

"You steady her from the side while I lift and push her in."

Kelsey went to the side of the board and did as Jordon instructed.

He shook his head, removing the water from his soaked hair. "Okay, let's get her in,"

With muscles straining, Kelsey held the slippery board in place the best she could. Finally, Jordon gave a last push and Molly went in as far as the front seat would allow. Hardy barked as they worked.

"I'm going to ride with her," Kelsey lifted her knee to climb in. Strong hands lifted her and placed her inside. She crawled to Molly's head.

Jordon closed one of the doors but the other wouldn't shut. Pulling off his belt he wrapped it through the door handles and secured it. "That should hold until we get to the hospital. Hardy, go home," he said in a firm tone.

Hardy gave one last bark.

Jordon disappeared from her sight and seconds later the SUV was running. Tires spun in the wet grass then hit shell and crunched before they found pavement.

Kelsey held on to the board, steadying it, as Jordon drove through the obstacle course on the roads to the hospital. During the drive he was on the phone, letting the E.R. know that they were coming and the status of Molly's injuries. The trip seem to take hours when it couldn't have been more than ten minutes.

Jordon wheeled the large SUV under the light of the E.R. cover, honked a couple of times and pulled to a stop. Seconds later he was at the doors and the E.R. staff arrived with a gurney.

They placed Molly, surfboard and all, on the rolling bed. As she was being pushed into the hospital, Kelsey moved to the back of the SUV and Jordon helped her out. He put his arm around her shoulders and squeezed. "You did great. I've got to move the SUV. I'll be there in a minute."

Kelsey was headed inside as he pulled away. Rushing to the cubicle where they were working on Molly, Kelsey stood in the hall out of the way. Jordon joined her, standing behind her and placing a supportive hand on her waist. She leaned back against him appreciating his sturdy company. She shuddered. Without him, Molly might have died under that tree.

"Hang in there," he whispered in her ear.

One of the surgeons looked at them. "Your diagnosis was spot on, Jordon. Internal bleeding. The spleen will have to come out. Maybe a little patchwork. I'll know more when I get in there."

Kelsey slumped against Jordon. He brought his hand further around her waist and tightened it.

"We'll be in the waiting room," he said.

The surgeon nodded and went back to Molly.

"I need to call her parents." Kelsey searched her pocket for her cell. "It must be in your SUV."

Jordon pulled out his phone. "What's the number?"

As Kelsey called it out he punched it into the phone then handed it to her. Kelsey's heart was in her throat as she waited to hear one of Molly's parent's voices. Her mother answered and Kelsey explained what had happened and that Molly was in surgery. A minute later Kelsey ended the call.

"They're on their way."

"Good. Come on. We're going to the doctor's overnight room to get a shower and dry clothes. Then let's find ourselves a hot meal."

Kelsey opened her mouth to argue.

"Molly's in good hands and you can't be here for her if you don't take care of yourself."

She let Jordon lead her through the E.R. to the doctor's sleep room. She'd never been inside. Jordon shut the door behind them. He stepped into the bath and the sound of water filled the space.

Returning with a towel in his hand, he said, "You go

get a shower." He started rubbing his hair. "Don't take too long or I'll be in to join you."

Kelsey didn't hesitate before she entered the small room and closed the door.

Jordon was confident it would take him days, possibly weeks before his muscles would quit screaming. Every time he moved his body protested. He kicked off his shoes, pulled his wet shirt off and dropped it on the floor with a slosh. Next went his pants and underwear. He wrapped the towel around his hips and turned on the TV. The weather channel announcer stood in front of a map. The swath of color across the Gulf area indicated Golden Shores was in for a few more hours of rain.

The sound of the water being turned off reminded him that Kelsey was but a few feet away and nude. She'd been amazing over the last few hours. There hadn't been a single complaint from her. She'd followed his directions to the letter and had been brilliant in thinking of the surfboard. He couldn't have asked for a more able and industrious person to have as a partner during an emergency.

The door of the bath opened, letting out a cloud of steam. His breath caught. Kelsey's hair stood on end and the white towel contrasted with her late-summer tan. His manhood stirred. This wasn't the time or the place. If it were, he'd pull the towel off her, bring those gorgeous curves against him and make use of the single bed inches away.

"There are scrubs…" he cleared his throat "…in the bottom drawer of that chest." He pointed to the cabinet the TV sat on.

She moved out of the doorway. He stepped beyond her, making sure he didn't touch her, and closed the door behind him with a firm click. If he didn't get away from her soon, he wouldn't go at all.

Safe behind the door, he turned the water on. It was still running hot from her shower but he switched it to cold and stepped in. He didn't linger in the shower but Kelsey wasn't in the room when he came out.

Would he always have to hunt her down? Pretty sure where she was, he headed for the surgery waiting room. She sat curled in a chair with her head in her hands, shoulders shaking. It had been a rough enough night, caring for patients, but to add her roommate being crushed under a tree and being part of the rescue effort had taken its toll. It was too much for almost anyone. Even someone as strong as Kelsey. Going to her, he wrapped an arm around her and pulled her to him. She didn't resist. Instead, she buried her head in his shoulder and let the tears flow.

For long moments he sat with her crying in his arms as his hands glided along her back in an effort to soothe her. He hadn't heard a woman cry since his mother had said goodbye when he'd been sixteen. He'd refused to look at her and he hadn't let her tears affect him then. Now his heart hurt for Kelsey. How had Kelsey succeeded in getting to him so much? She wasn't even his type. Still, when that limb had been about to fall on her, he hadn't even stopped to think about grabbing her.

"When Molly's out of the woods, you can go home and get some rest."

"I don't have a home. There's a tree in it." She cried softly.

He hadn't known her long but she had to be at the end of her rope if she was feeling sorry for herself.

"Aw, sweetie, it's going to be fine."

He continued to hold her close. Kelsey settled and drooped against his chest. She was asleep. Something about having her in his arms felt right, even though he wanted nothing to do with a woman.

Kelsey woke to the sound of two male voices. One rumbled beneath her ear and the other was speaking above her. Her eyes blinked open and she sat up, pushing against the hard torso beneath her.

She looked at the surgeon dressed in blue scrubs. "Is Molly all right?"

Jordon released her and she sat up. She missed his warmth and security immediately.

"I had to remove Molly's spleen and repair a few ruptures in her intestines. She is still unconscious, so we don't know yet about any brain damage. We'll just have to wait and see. She'll be in Recovery for another hour or two and then in ICU. You need to go home and get some rest. You can see her later this evening."

Jordon stood. "Thanks. I'll see about Kelsey. We'll be back later."

The surgeon nodded and walked through the swinging doors and back into the surgical wing.

Where did Jordon get off, deciding what she was going to do? No man was going to take over her life. She'd had enough of that when she'd been a kid.

"I'm staying here."

Jordon frowned at her as if she'd this instant proclaimed she was a mermaid.

"No, you're not. You need rest and you're doing Molly no good here. You can call and check on her."

"I'm fine here."

"What eats you so much about me telling you to do something that is only in your best interest?"

"I don't like to be told what to do."

"This time you'll just have to get over it." He leaned

down and said in a low forbidding voice, "I'm taking you out of this hospital by choice or force. It's your decision but you're leaving."

Kelsey gulped.

"I don't have to do what you say."

"No, you don't. But you're not being rational right now and since I'm the only one here in his right mind, I'm making the decisions. So what will it be? Over my shoulder or on your own two feet?"

He sounded like he meant it. Kelsey jumped up and stomped down the hallway toward the exit. She was being childish, but she had worked so hard to get out from under her father's iron hand and her mother's obliviousness. Kelsey didn't want to go back there any time, for anyone. Still, she was almost at her breaking point after no sleep for twenty-four hours, the adrenaline rush of finding Molly and now the waiting.

"Where're you headed?" Jordon's deep voice asked in a tone of a person speaking to a child.

"Home, like you told me to."

"And how're you going to get there?"

She stopped and narrowed her eyes at him. "In my car."

"So your little car is going to make it over the tree in the road and you're going to cuddle up in your wet bed under the tree."

"You seem to have all the answers. What do you think I should do?"

Without blinking an eye or pausing, he said, "Come home with me."

Even Jordon looked stricken for a second at his statement.

"Why would I do that?"

"Do you have somewhere else you would rather go?"

Anywhere else came to mind.

"Maybe your sister's? I'll be glad to see that you get there."

To China's? No. She and Payton had worked at the clinic like Jordon and she had at the hospital. China didn't need her around. She needed to rest. There was a baby to think about now. Kelsey wouldn't go to her parents'. That wasn't even an option.

"Okay. But I'm only on the sofa until this evening then I'll find a place to stay until my house is repaired."

"For once you're being sensible."

She didn't like the sound of satisfaction in his voice.

"We need to go and get something to eat then pick up our sack of wet clothes." He passed her, going in the direction of the cafeteria.

Kelsey followed a couple of paces behind, still not in complete agreement with the plans. They shared a quiet meal eating at a two-person table in the far corner of the large room.

"You want anything else?" Jordon asked, when her plate was clean.

Kelsey shook her head. She would've said she couldn't have eaten anything but she'd had a big meal and was glad for it.

"Good." He pushed his chair back. "Then let's go get those clothes and then get some sleep. I'm beat. I know you must be also."

She waited outside the doctor's sleep room while he gathered their clothes. There was something far too intimate about their clothes being commingled in the plastic bag Jordon carried.

How had her life become so entangled with his?

A little later Kelsey climbed out of the SUV when Jordon stopped in his drive. It was daylight but still gloomy and rainy. Even that had become a more steady flow instead of a frog strangler. Hardy came out of a doghouse that sat at the rear of the house. Wagging his tail, he greeted her first then went around to where Jordon was pulling their clothes out of the backseat.

With the bag in hand, he head toward the door. Kelsey moved across the yard toward her place.

"Where're you going?" The exasperation in his voice would have been comical under other circumstances.

"I'm going to my house to get some clothes and personal things."

"You can't do that. It isn't safe."

"Maybe not, but you can't stop me."

Jordon dropped the bag and stalked toward her. "Okay, you have ten minutes to get what you can. After that I haul you out."

"Don't tell me what to do!"

He put up a defensive hand. "Okay, okay. I'll help you for as long as it takes. Be careful. And for both our sakes, work fast. You don't know if the roof could fall in at any time."

"You didn't make a big deal of that when we were getting Molly out."

"I didn't want to scare you and we had no choice then. Are you always so unreasonable when you're tired?"

Kelsey chose to ignore the question and kept walking. She opened the door to her house and looked around. In the daylight it looked even worse. She blinked back the tears that threatened. It could have been worse. Molly could be dead. Squaring her shoulders, she found a black plastic garbage bag under the kitchen counter and weaved her way through the top of the tree to her bedroom. Memories of following this path in the dark made her shudder.

Jordon remained close behind her, like a guardian angel. He waited at the door while she entered the bedroom. The floor was wet. She touched the bed and found it damp also. Jordon was right—she couldn't have stayed here. Going to her chest of drawers, she grabbed fistfuls of clothing and stuffed them into the bag. Having emptied the drawers, she went to the closet and took what clothes she could until the bag was full.

Jordon stepped forward and said, "I'll take that."

She let him have it. Was the relieved look that crossed his face been because she hadn't argued? Maybe she had been overreacting.

A creaking from above made her glance up.

"We need to get moving," Jordon said with a firm tone of urgency.

"I have to get my jewelry box." She went to her dresser and picked up the square wooden box sitting there and pulled it to her chest. "I'm ready."

Without a word, Jordon turned and walked down the hall. With one quick glance at the room, Kelsey followed. Soon they were out of the gloomy house and walking toward Jordon's.

"You were a great help this morning. The surfboard was inspired."

"Thanks." She met his gaze for a second. "I'm sorry I haven't said thank you sooner. I'm glad you were with me when we found Molly. She's alive because of you."

"I'm not sure about that, but I do appreciate the vote of confidence."

Hardy joined them.

"And you, boy, were great also." She looked at Jordon. "How did you know Hardy would find her?"

"Because he was in training to be a rescue dog before I got him. He washed out because he couldn't focus."

"Well, your focus was perfect this morning." She patted the dog on the head.

Jordon's liked Kelsey's praise. It was much nicer than her anger and indignation. Had he been so high handed to warrant her reaction when he'd said she needed to get some rest? Had an old boyfriend made her so defensive? If he remembered right, her father had been tough. Maybe it was a reaction from that.

He pushed his door open and held the screen, letting Kelsey and Hardy enter first. She wandered around the room as if surveying it all then headed for the sofa, placing the box she'd been clutching to her chest on the end table.

"I'll take care of washing the clothes after I've had a nap." She lay down on the sofa, curled up and was fast asleep almost instantly.

Jordon looked at her in amazement. He had never seen someone go out like a light before. Kelsey was exhausted in mind, body and spirit. He started the clothes washing then went to his bedroom and pulled the covers back on the bed before returning to the living room. Looking down at Kelsey, he found that even with her short hair in disarray she was quite striking. Her skin looked creamy. Unable to resist a touch, he ran a finger along one silky cheek. She sighed.

Gently, in order not to wake her, he slipped her shoes off, letting them fall to the floor. Lifting her into his arms and cradling her against his chest, he stood. She felt warm and perfect but he had to push those feelings away. Kelsey was the type of woman who would break his heart.

She cuddled against him, making her more difficult to resist. Gritting his teeth and with rock-hard control, he carried her to his bed and placed her on it. He covered her and tucked her in. She made a soft mumble and settled in, pulling his pillow to her. Jordon wished it was him. He would have to wash the bedclothes and remove her scent or he'd never get another good night's sleep.

Against his better judgment and all his efforts not to, he was falling for the woman. At the door, he looked back at her snuggled in as if she belonged there. The problem was, he wasn't with her.

Kelsey woke to darkness. She pushed against the tree leaves that surrounded her face before she realized it was the blanket around her.

She inhaled deeply.

Jordon.

Where was she? That's right, she was at his house. Where was he? She'd fallen asleep on the sofa. How had she gotten here? Had he carried her?

She turned on the bedside table lamp and looked around the room. Thank goodness Jordon wasn't with her. She was becoming far too dependent on him, growing to like having his support. He had been wonderful the night before with Molly. Even when *she* had broken down in tears. For once she'd found his high-handedness comforting.

When she'd first seen the house she'd wanted to scream. There she'd felt like she'd had a real home for the first time since Chad had left. Now it was destroyed.

Her gaze circled the room. It was masculine with unfinished wood for the walls, dark furniture and a massive bed. It was Jordon's room. Jordon's bed. One she needed to get out of.

Tossing the covers away, she stood and groaned. Her back and leg muscles were complaining. She rolled her shoulders in the hope of easing the aches but it didn't help. All the physical activity of the morning had gotten to her.

It was pitch black outside. Kelsey looked at the clock.

It was ten-fifteen at night. She'd slept the day away and missed visiting hours. She needed to call and check on Molly.

Glancing down, she saw she still wore the scrubs she'd put on at the hospital. What she wouldn't give for a long bath and her own clothes. Her stomach made a loud unsociable noise. And some food.

But first she needed to find Jordon. Tiptoeing down the hall, she found another room. It had been made into a study but there were still boxes stacked in the corner as if Jordon hadn't completely unpacked. Continuing toward the front of the house to the living area, she saw Jordon curled up on the sofa, which was much too small for his large frame.

Hardy lay on the floor beside him. The dog looked up at her. She put a finger to her lips and shushed him. The blanket that Jordon must have pulled over him had slipped to the floor. She picked it up and covered him with it. He shifted and rolled over.

He'd been her hero yesterday. What would it be like to lean over and kiss the stubble-covered jaw? Would it be as firm as it looked? Would he mind if she did?

Mentally shaking her head, Kelsey stepped away before she was tempted further. She tried to remember why she was there. Where had she'd last seen her phone? She'd been with Molly. Jordon's SUV. Making an effort not to wake Jordon, she went outside with Hardy at her heels. On bare feet she walked across the wet grass. Opening the back door of the SUV, she climb in and ran her hands around in search of the phone. She located it sandwiched between the folded seat and seat-belt holder. Her heart sank when she saw that the battery was dead.

A deep voice behind her said, "Fine thanks I get for giving a homeless woman my bed. She sneaks off without saying a word."

Kelsey shrieked and lurched upward, hitting her head on the roof of the vehicle.

"And a concussion," she mumbled, as she sat down and rubbed her skull.

"Are you okay?" His voice turned solemn with concern. "Let me have a look."

"I'm fine. I've just got a small knot." She scooted on her butt, feet first, out the door.

"I didn't mean to scare you."

Jordon hadn't sounded this worried even when they'd found Molly. "I'm fine. Really. It takes more than a bump on the head to get me down."

"I know. I've seen you in action. What're you doing out here anyway?"

"I was looking for my phone." He waited as if expecting her to say more. "I left it in here when we took Molly to the hospital." She climbed out of the SUV and faced him. "Really, I was out here, trying to hot-wire your SUV," she said sarcastically, "but I was afraid Hardy might wake you." She patted Hardy's neck.

"Funny. It would have been smarter to take the keys. Did you find your phone?" Jordon closed the doors to the vehicle.

"I did but the battery is dead. Can I use yours to call the hospital?"

"Already did that. Molly is holding her own but still in guarded condition."

Kelsey lips quivered and she pressed them together to keep from crying.

As if Jordon knew the news had upset her he put his arm across her shoulders and led her across the yard. "Hang in there. Molly's young and strong. She'll get through this."

The need to be held filled her. She wanted another human's warm touch, to forget how horrible it was to see her friend pinned under that tree. Jordon was who she wanted. To absorb his strength, have his reassurance. To be kissed, and return that kiss. She wrapped her arms around his waist and pulled him closer, laying her head against his firm chest as they walked toward the house.

CHAPTER SIX

JORDON WASN'T SURE what Kelsey's actions meant. He knew what he wished they indicated but he'd misread her a number of times and he sure hoped he wasn't doing so one more time. To begin with, he'd seen her as nothing but a teasing gadfly but Kelsey had proved there was more to her than a good-time girl. Maybe she just wanted a friend to see her through a tough time.

His arms tightened, pulling her closer then eased long enough to let her move past him through the door into the house. She brushed his chest as she went by, making his desire grow. Plenty of women had touched him on purpose and his body had never gone on the high alert he was experiencing now. Hardy followed close behind. Even his dog seemed enamored by Kelsey.

Jordon stepped inside. The living room was dark except for one small reading lamp he'd turned on when he'd woken.

Kelsey stood at the end of the kitchen bar, facing him. Hardy sat at her feet. Her gaze locked with his. What was going on? His emotions were like being on a swing bridge, unsteady and unfamiliar, fearing the next step might be the wrong one.

Jordon raised a brow then turned to close the door. He needed a few seconds to gain control. He felt more than heard Kelsey step nearer. Returning round, his breath caught as she stretched upward on her toes and kissed him. It was too brief, but it was the sweetest kiss he'd ever received. He wanted more. More kisses. More of her.

"What was that for?" His voice was raspy leaving him embarrassed. He cleared his throat.

"Really? Aren't you a little old not to know when a woman wants you?"

Her eyes held a dark come-hither look. "With you it's hard to tell. You run hot and cold too often."

She stepped closer, pressing her body against his. "I'm feeling rather hot at the moment."

Jordon growled low in his throat. He'd been approached by women before but this blatant come-on from Kelsey was the sexist. "Hey, I'm not complaining here. And I'm no superhero who's going to turn a beautiful sexy woman down, but what has changed your mind about me?"

"You were my hero yesterday." Her breath was so soft against his lips that he almost missed what she said. She wrapped her arms around his neck and pulled his mouth down to meet hers.

He groaned and circled her waist, bringing her tightly against him.

Her tongue teased his lips until he opened for her. She made a suggestive rub against him, making his desire soar and his manhood grow rigid. Her tongue met his, moved away and returned to caress his another time.

Had he ever been this turned on? He took control of the kiss, taking it deeper. She pulled away. He wanted to complain, demand she return to kissing him, but he got caught up in the movement of her lips across his cheek to his ear. She took his earlobe between her teeth and nipped, then tugged, making low cooing sounds.

The woman was killing him.

Her fingers burrowed through his hair as her lips returned to his.

Yes, this was more than he'd imagine in the middle of the night when he'd dreamed of her. Jordon pulled away and gazed down at her. "I don't know if this is a post-traumatic reaction or not but there's no going back from here."

"I'm no longer twelve so why don't you hush and stop being the chivalrous hero and take me to bed? I want to forget everything but how you make me feel."

He crushed her mouth with his, then scooped her up over his shoulder and carried her down the hall. Leaning over, he let her fall back on to the bed with a flop before pinning her body beneath his.

Kelsey shifted beneath him, creating further intimacy. "Mmm, I like this."

She cupped his face and guided his mouth to hers close enough that the tip of her tongue tormented him before she opened and accepted his entrance.

His hands went to her back and he lifted her against him, grinding his hips into her. There was too much between them. Too much need, too much heat and too many clothes.

He pushed the cotton material of her scrub top up. She wore no bra. It was in the washer where he'd put it earlier. With regret, he released her lips and pulled away. He rolled to his side then gathered the material of her top in both hands and pulled. "This has to come off."

Kelsey arched her back and raised her arms over her head, helping him. With her arms still half in and half out of the shirt, her glorious breasts were available for his viewing pleasure and he planned to take full advantage. He clasped her hands and held them in one of his.

His mouth watered as he lowered inch by inch to surround one rosy straining nipple. Could anything be this wonderful? Giving the erect tip a tug, he was rewarded with a buck of her hips. Kelsey's uninhibited reaction fueled his already raging desire. She was sunshine, sensuality and sweetness. He wanted to bask in it, feel it and taste it until his heart was content.

Jordon laid a leg across one of hers, holding her in place, making her a smorgasbord of delights displayed for him alone. Sucking at her nipple again then sweeping his tongue around it, he was rewarded with a moan. She was so responsive, accepting. His length strained and throbbed. He placed his hand on her flat stomach, spreading his fingers wide. Her skin beneath his hands was pure silk.

Kelsey trembled. The self-assured and in-control Kelsey was like putty in his hands. He'd never felt more of a man. As he moved his mouth away from one breast to the other, his gaze met her half-lidded one. Her crimson-colored mouth was partially open and a dreamy look covered her face. If he hadn't by this time been hot for her, that look of heavenly pleasure would have made him so. She was breathtaking.

Using his index finger, he twirled it around her belly button at the same time he pulled her nipple into his mouth. She arched, offering him the world. He couldn't have turned it down even if he'd wanted to, and he didn't. His hand traveled over the heated skin of her stomach to cup one breast. He hadn't been wrong. They were flawless.

"I want to touch you." His words sounded coarse with need.

She tried to sit.

Grinning, he shook his head in slow motion one way and then the other. "For once you're not running the show." Jordon lifted, kneaded and kissed her breast until she moaned for mercy. Capturing the sound with his mouth, he released her wrists. He needed her touch.

Kelsey shook her shirt away and her hands found his T-shirt, her fingers clawing to pull it up. His breath caught when her hands slid under the material and touched his skin. Yanking until he had no choice but to stop kissing her and remove his shirt, she helped him off with it then threw it to the floor. Kelsey sighed as his lips found hers again and her chest met his. The touch of her skin against his almost did him in. Jordon ran his hand down low over her belly.

She shivered.

"Like that, do you?" He watched her skin ripple as his hand traveled across her satiny surface. He brought his hand back and followed the same path again. She squirmed. His fingers crept toward the place he desired the most, this time sliding under her elastic waistband. His breath caught. She wore no panties. Those must have been tied up in her other clothes he'd put in the wash.

Kelsey sucked in a breath as he raked over her mound and retreated.

Jordon leaned forward and kissed her where her pants met skin, running small nipping kisses along that line.

Her fingers curled in his hair.

Jordon pushed away her pants until what had been hidden was revealed.

She kicked the scrub pants off and pulled at his shoulders. "I want—"

"Shush, sweetie. I have to admire you."

Her long supple legs, tanned from the sun, were spread out before him, waiting to pull him to her. He moved his hand across her springy curls to cup her. With a measured movement he slid a finger to her center, finding it damp and hot.

She clenched his finger.

He looked at her face.

Kelsey's eyes were closed tight and her shoulders curled forward. As the tenseness eased from her body, a look of pure bliss covered her face and she settled to the bed. Her eyes opened and her soft gaze met his for a second before her lids fluttered closed.

Jordon's chest swelled. How had the woman managed to make him feel like beating his chest when he hadn't even entered her?

What had just happened? Jordon had made her come with the simple touch of his finger.

Kelsey had always maintained the lead in her relationships. That way they wouldn't get out of hand. This time she'd lost it. Given it over to Jordon and had enjoyed every perfect minute. What was the man doing to her?

She opened her eyes to find him studying her with the smile of a male who knew he'd done something amazing.

"Thanks. That was nice." She ran a hand down his chest, enjoying the feel of hair over firm pectoral muscles.

"You're welcome." His lips curled into a self-satisfied grin.

She leaned up and reached for the clasp of his jeans. "How about joining me this time?"

"I do believe I will."

One of the things she liked best about Jordon was his wit. Other men she'd been with had been so serious. They had been more interested in themselves than her pleasure. Minutes ago it had been all about her. She'd come to believe that it would never be about what she wanted or needed, but Jordon had proved her wrong.

Her hand wandered over his zipper and the large bulge beneath. Jordon audibly took in a breath. So she still had some power.

He pushed her hand away and rose. Shucking his pants,

he let them drop to the floor. Jordon made her stare in amazement as he stood in all his bold and masculine glory before her. He opened the drawer of the bedside table and pulled out a foil packet. Tearing it, he covered himself.

With the look of a prowling cat that wouldn't let his prey escape, he joined her on the bed again. Nudging her back against the covers, his hair-roughened legs found their place between her legs. His hands came to cup her breast and lift them to his moist mouth. Her womb contracted in unison with each tug and pull, making her squirm with building need. She opened her mouth to complain and Jordon brought his down to meet hers. The tip of his length kissed her throbbing center.

Her fingertips massaged the skin at his waist, urging him to take her. She deepened their kiss, tangling her tongue with his while lifting her center in offering.

With the growl of a man who had held back as long as he could, Jordon thrust forward, filling her. He stilled. Then pulled back to a point she feared he'd leave. With exquisite control, he reentered her, drawing back again and again until the towering, swirling need took her and released her into a floating abyss of pleasure. Three deep plunges later, Jordon tensed and groaned his completion.

He rolled from her but his index finger touched her thigh as if he wanted to maintain their connection.

"J-man, that was nice."

Their breathing slowed in unison, something that both amazed her and sent a zing of fear through her. What was happening here? She needed to distance herself, regain some equilibrium. He turned on his side, facing her. "J-man? I haven't been called that in years."

She pushed off the bed, picking up the first thing she could use to cover herself, which turned out to be Jordon's shirt. "Remember when you used to come to my house?"

He sat beside her on the edge of the bed. "In those days I was either high or thinking about getting high. I don't remember much."

A ripple of disappointment went through her. Yet she'd still noticed a note of pain in his voice that Kelsey didn't quite understand. "I guess it's unrealistic to think you would remember someone's kid sister."

The tip of his finger grazed the length of her thigh. "I'll never forget you again."

His sexy grin made her middle turn to mush. She wanted him. For once she wasn't thinking of how she'd get out of this as soon as possible without hurting his feelings. That was something that had never happened before. She'd always seen to it that she didn't linger.

Jordon gave her a long, deep kiss. "How about we make some more memories?"

Kelsey had taken command of their lovemaking and Jordon had never been more turned on, or had a more mind-blowing release. Even now he was growing stiff, thinking of her above him.

Kelsey stirred and rubbed catlike against him. She turned and looked up at him. "Hey."

"Hi."

"I've been wondering…"

He was afraid of what might be said next. "If I know how to cook?"

She grinned. "My guess would be that you do, but that isn't it. I want to know where you and Chad went."

This wasn't what he'd expected. "When?"

"When you left."

"*We* didn't go anywhere. My father enrolled me in military school in Virginia and I left the morning I got out of jail."

"Oh." She opened her mouth to say something then closed it.

He waited, wanting to change the subject but knowing she wouldn't let him. He had to face the music. This conversation had been a long time coming.

"Do you know where Chad went?" More softly, she continued, "Where he is? If he's alive?"

There was the question he dreaded. "I haven't seen him in some time." At least that was an honest answer, of sorts.

The hope died in her eyes. Jordon's chest contracted. It was worse than he'd believed. He wasn't feeling heroic at all now.

It almost destroyed him but he had to keep his word. He'd promised Chad not to tell anyone, his parents or sisters in particular, that he was in prison. Jordon had thought nothing of the promise at the time, never imagining that he'd meet any of Chad's family again, much less become involved with one of his sisters. And involved Jordon was. Far too much so. If he allowed his feelings to go much further he was afraid he might fall in love with Kelsey.

The first chance he had he was going to visit Chad. He had to allow him to tell his family he was at least alive.

"When was the last time you saw Chad?"

"The morning after you both got into trouble."

"Really?"

"He left and we thought he was with you." She turned to look at him. "We haven't heard from him in fifteen years, three months and twenty-one days."

Chad hadn't said he'd never contacted his family. That explained some of how she felt about her parents. "You blame your parents, don't you?"

She looked away toward a picture of a fishing boat that hung on the wall. "Yeah."

"Will you tell me about it?" he asked softly.

"I don't talk about it."

"I figured as much. You haven't looked at your parents' house once when we were riding by except after the storm." For a few seconds he wasn't sure she would say any more.

She didn't look at him as she said in a tight voice, "My father was so inflexible about what we could and couldn't do. I idolized Chad. It almost killed me when he left. I can't stand the thought that he might be dead or that he was alone if he did die."

Jordon's heart constricted. He opened his mouth to tell her that Chad was alive but he couldn't. He'd given his word. That meant something to him. He'd learned the value of trust when his mother had run around on his father. Had had it driven home again when his ex had not only crushed his heart but had taken his professional integrity also. No, giving his word was too important, that bond of trust unbreakable. He wouldn't discard his commitment to Chad, not even for Kelsey.

"That had to have been tough."

"Yeah. That's an understatement. My parents drove Chad away. I made up my mind to leave home as soon as I could. I pretty much bided my time until I could get out of there. China covered for me when I became the wild child my parents feared. 'You're no better than your brother,' I heard on more than one occasion when China couldn't make what I'd done go away soon enough."

"Like what?"

"The usual stuff. Sneaking out at night, smoking, seeing boys they didn't like. They thought it, so I did it."

That explained her reputation. "You were determined to get back at them."

"I guess I was. I couldn't believe my father could tell someone he said he loved to leave. And my mother was worse, she stood by and said nothing. When I turned sixteen I got a job, and saved my money. I was out of there the day I turned eighteen."

And that explained her independence. Her need to control. She'd even worked to build a surrogate family by being the person who planned events, surrounding herself with people. "I'm impressed. To be on your own at that young an age. Then get an education."

"Hey, don't make me out as a wonder woman. I made some poor choices, lived with the wrong guy, slept on a friend's floor for months before I decided if I wanted to get out of Golden Shores I needed to find a way to do that. I remember my high school counselor telling me about an educational program the hospital offered. They would send me to school, and I'd owe them X number of years."

Jordon sucked in air as if he'd been punched. He'd forgotten. She was planning to move. The thought of Kelsey no longer being around made him want to grab her and hold on. He was stepping over a line. He'd no intention of letting her matter that much.

"And now you've paid your time, hence the job in Atlanta."

The light of a person seeing a beautiful possibility within their grasp filled her eyes. "Yes, it's my chance to leave my parents, my less than stellar past behind and start fresh. What I hate most about leaving is not seeing China regularly but she has Payton and the baby. We'll visit."

Where did that leave him? Here, now, making the most of what time he had. Reaching for Kelsey's hand, he pulled her to him. She resisted for a second then slid along him. Looking into her eyes as his hands skimmed over her bottom, he lifted her until she straddled him. "Then we don't have any time to waste."

Pleasurable minutes later, Kelsey lay wrapped in his

arms. Jordon pulled the covers over them and clicked off the light. Kelsey nestled against him, putting her head on his shoulder.

The sun was but a pink haze in the eastern sky when Jordon woke again with a warm bare behind settled against him. Life was good. What were his chances of having Kelsey in his bed nightly? Everything about her said it wouldn't be as easy as asking. He'd have to smooth-talk her, charm her before she'd give in, but she would give in. She had to for his sake.

"Tell me what happened."

Jordon started. She was awake. He knew what she referred to but he didn't want to spend their time together talking about the past.

"Good morning to you too."

She shifted to face him. "Tell me about military school."

At least she wasn't asking about his mother. "I went kicking and screaming. It was that or Dad was going to let me stay in jail. He called in a favor otherwise the school would have never taken me. Dad got a transfer so he'd be close enough that I could at least spend holidays with him."

She wrinkled her nose and asked, "Where was your mother?"

"She and Dad divorced two years before. She'd moved to California." He didn't even try to keep the bitterness from his voice.

"You haven't seen her since, have you?"

Was he that easy to read? "No."

"Why not?"

"I don't want to go into it."

"You going to military school rather than running away to live with your mother says something. Okay, if you won't tell me about that, then tell me about how you decided to become a doctor."

"You're not going to give up on the questions, are you?"

She rolled over and faced him, putting an arm on his chest. "Nope. You know about me, but I don't know much about you. So spill. I want to know it all."

"Despite my unlawful ways, I managed to keep my grades up in school. The first few months in military school were tough. I stayed in trouble, on the verge of being thrown out almost daily."

"So did you get thrown out?"

"No." For that he would be forever grateful.

"What happened?" She looked at him intently.

"One night I was sneaking in and got caught by an old sergeant who had lost his arm. He sat me down and told me about his life and how I was throwing mine away. He'd lost his arm doing something foolish and he regretted it every day. I may not have lost an arm but I might lose more if I didn't get my act together. I spent all my spare time after that with him."

"So how did you decide to be a doctor?"

"I had always wanted to be a doctor. I liked helping people. Enough talk about me."

He brought his hand to rest on her hip and nudged her closer.

Kelsey pushed his hand away.

"Nope. I've got one more question."

Jordon groaned.

"I want to know why you decided to move back here."

He tensed. His gut roiled. She really was hitting all the sore spots. If it wasn't for her unwavering gaze and the value he placed on truth he might have told her something less honest just to get off the subject. But he couldn't.

"Okay, if you really want to know. My partner was convicted of Medicaid fraud. I wasn't involved but I was close enough that my records were looked into." He broke their gaze. No longer speaking to her, he said as if in a vacuum, "I stood beside my partner but it killed all my credibility. To make it worse, we were engaged. I believed in her, trusted her. I don't ever want a relationship like that again." The pain and bitterness flowed through him like the first second he'd learned of her deceit. "There wasn't much left for me to do but to start over. I thought this would be a good place to do so."

Kelsey placed hand on his chest palm down and said in a soothing voice, "I'm sorry. That had to have been tough."

"It was." Somehow he felt better for just saying it out loud. As if he'd thrown off the ugliness of the past to truly start living in the here and now.

"Thanks for telling me. I understand your reaction to some things now." She hugged him and then scooted off the bed. "I'm sorry that happened to you. I understand how you feel the way you do."

"Where're you going? It's still early."

Jordon had never seen anything more beautiful than Kelsey standing there in her full glory in the buttery light of morning. She was bodacious, confident and alluring. An amazing combination. He wanted it all for himself.

"I need to check on Molly. See about my house." She rifled through the sack that held her clothes, pulling items from it. "Mind if I use your shower?"

She seemed to be pulling away. Had his comment about never wanting a relationship like the one he'd had with his ex made Kelsey think he did want something more with her? "No. Mind if I share? I'll dress and go with you."

"That's not necessary." She didn't even look back at him.

Jordon sat on the side of the bed. Kelsey acted as if the amazing night they'd shared meant nothing. He refused to be dismissed so easily.

"Kelsey, do you mind looking at me?"

Instead of doing so, she took her armload of clothes and headed toward the bath.

"Kelsey!"

She stopped short and whirled round to face him. "Don't you ever shout at me!"

"Hey, I'm sorry. I was just trying to get your attention. I'd like to know what's going on." He found his pants and pulled them on.

"Going on?" She looked at him in disbelief. "One, my best friend is in the hospital and I don't know how badly off she is and, two, I don't have a house anymore, which means I don't have a place to stay. So now you know what's going on."

"You know that isn't what I was talking about." Jordon stepped toward her.

"What else is there to talk about?"

"Us."

She looked at him directly. "Jordon, there is no us."

"Seemed to me there was plenty of us last night."

"Last night was about nerves, adrenaline. Right place at the right time."

Had he been slapped in the face? He'd said similar words to women before, had seen the looks on their faces. That must be on his now but this was the first time he been on the receiving end of a brush-off. He didn't like it and refused to accept it.

"That's cold even for you, Kelsey." A niggle of satisfaction went through him at her slight flinch.

"Look, Jordon, the sex was amazing, you were amazing, but I'm leaving Golden Shores as soon as the job in Atlanta opens up. I'm not going to start a relationship knowing that I'm leaving. You don't want one either. After what you said about your ex I can't blame you. I don't think it's wise for either of us go any further than this."

Jordon stepped into her personal space. She didn't budge. That was the Kelsey he knew well but after last night he was aware of her valuable side also. When she cared for someone she did so deeply, with all her heart and until the end.

"I'll tell you what. Why don't we forget about you leaving and enjoy the time we have until that happens? We're both adults. I believe we can handle that. We'll start with being friends."

"I don't know. Seems like after last night we might be stretching the meaning of the word 'friends' a bit."

Jordon pulled her into his arms, clothes and all, his hands finding the skin of her back. "Maybe so, but I don't mind if you don't." He kissed her.

Kelsey was confident that everything about being "friends" with Jordon was a bad idea. He wasn't the type of person a girl was only friends with. Even now, if it wasn't for wanting to see Molly, Kelsey would pull Jordon back into bed. She already liked him too much.

Leaving town was for her own sanity. She'd been controlled by her father and she wouldn't let Jordon manipulate her into something she didn't want to do. Still, she liked him. What would it hurt for them to spend some time together as long as they both knew the score?

She looked into his beautiful eyes. "Okay. But there have to be some rules."

"Like?" he drawled, as if he wasn't sure he liked the idea.

"Like you can't tell me what to do. You don't keep tabs on me. I go and do as I please without checking in with you. You understand I'm leaving town. That this stays on a friendly level, nothing more. No talk of us. No talk of love."

"And you're so sure I might fall in love with you."

"I don't know but I don't want it to happen."

"No worries there. Having a good time is all I'm interested in. I've had the other and it wasn't pleasant when it ended."

"I wouldn't have done you that way."

"I know that but you can't blame a guy for being gun shy."

There was a sharp squeeze in the area of her chest. All of a sudden she didn't like being just a good time for Jordon. She wanted to mean more but she refused to say that. "It's a deal."

He grinned. "Then I think we should seal it with a kiss." His lips met hers. She let go of the clothes, letting them drop between them, and wrapped her arms around his neck, returning his kiss. Jordon lifted her and carried her in the direction of the bath.

There he put her down long enough to turn on the water. Stepping into the shower, he pulled her after him. She shrieked as the cool water touched her heated skin. Jordon chuckled before he picked her up again and she wrapped her legs around his waist. "Cold? Don't worry, I'll heat you up."

His thick manhood stood between them, leaving her no reason to doubt him. He let her slide down his wet, slick body until he had fully entered her.

"Mmm, I like being friends with you," he murmured in her ear as he started to move. Kelsey closed her eyes and appreciated each thrust until she could stand it no longer. She found her pleasure and went weak against him. Supporting her against the tiles, he groaned in triumph against her neck.

Jordon guided her to her feet and helped her to stand. His eyes were still hooded with passion. "You know, this might be the nicest shower I've ever taken."

"And to think you haven't even picked up the soap yet."

Jordon gave her a light swat on the butt. "How like you to make fun after a wonderful moment."

She gave him a serious look. "I don't want you to forget we're only friends."

"You sure know how to hurt a man's ego. The least you could do is say thank you."

She cupped his face. "Last night was wonderful. A second ago was so amazing my knees are still weak. Thank you, Jordon." She kissed him with all that she felt, which was far more than she wanted to.

When they came up for air, Jordon said, "That's more like it."

Kelsey couldn't help but grin. In that moment he reminded her so much of the boy she'd had such a crush on. Now she had a crush on the man.

He picked up a bar of soap. "I think we'd better focus on bathing so I can get you to the hospital to see Molly. I'll help you then you can help me." His voice was deep with suggestion.

Kelsey laughed. "I don't think that'll work."

She was right. Twenty minutes later they emerged from the bath. If she wasn't careful it would be her feelings she'd have to worry about when she left and not Jordon's.

Dressed in the few work clothes she had that weren't too wrinkled to wear, and almost ready to go to the hospital, she asked, "Hey, can I use your phone? I want to call and check on Molly."

"Sure."

Kelsey scooped up the phone off the bedside table where it had been through the night. She punched in the number and asked for ICU. Because Molly wasn't a family member, the clerk couldn't tell her anything except that Molly was still in guarded condition. Kelsey needed to see Molly for herself.

Kelsey searched the room. Where was her jewelry box?

"Problem?" Jordon asked, from where he was pulling socks out of a drawer.

"I thought I had brought my jewelry box in here."

"It's in the living room on the table beside the sofa."

"Yeah, that's right." She headed down the hall. Hardy met her in the kitchen and gave a yelp. "Hey, boy. Thanks for being a hero yesterday."

"Please don't make his head any larger," Jordon said, coming up behind her.

"There's nothing wrong in letting someone know they are appreciated."

"I thought that was what I was doing a few minutes ago."

Kelsey would have believed that she was beyond blushing but that was what she was doing. She didn't dare look at Jordon. Instead she said, "Any chance of getting a cup of coffee?"

"Sure," he said, and headed into the kitchen area.

While he was doing that she found her jewelry box. It had been the one thing she had taken with her when she had left her parents. Opening it, she checked to see if anything had been damaged. She looked over her shoulder to see where Jordon was. He had his back to her, pouring coffee. Lifting the tray and placing it on the table, she removed the picture of Chad that rested on top of the items below. It was damp but in good shape. Placing it to the side, she pushed the other items around with the end of her finger. Beneath some bracelets lay the yellow plastic ring that Jordon had given her long ago.

"Here you go," he said behind her.

Kelsey jumped. The box fell to the floor.

"Hey, I didn't mean to startle you."

She went down on her knees and turned the box upright. Jordon placed the cups on the nearby counter and joined her.

"I can get it," she assured him.

Jordon ignored her and continued to place necklaces, rings and bracelets into the box. When everything visible was returned, Kelsey picked up the box and set it on the table.

"This is Chad." Jordon's voice sounded pained.

She turned to find him holding her picture.

"I took it out of my parents' album. It's all I have left of him."

A stricken look fluttered through his eyes before he turned away from her. He bent down and reached a hand under the edge of the sofa. "Is this yours?"

In his palm lay the plastic ring.

Kelsey gulped. Would he remember that? He didn't remember her. She put out her hand. "It's mine."

His gaze met her as he picked up her hand and placed the ring on the third finger of her left hand just as he'd done when they'd been kids. "It looks like one of those rings out of a Cracker Jack box."

"It is. You gave it to me." Why had she said that? She pulled it off and dropped it in the box. Maybe it was time for him to remember.

"I did? When?"

"The night before you and Chad were arrested. I came into Chad's room and you were eating Cracker Jacks. You came out with the ring and put it on my finger. Said that now I was your girlfriend. Chad laughed and ran me out of the room."

Jordon stood then sat on a nearby stool that belonged to the kitchen bar. "Hey, I do remember that. You kept it all this time?"

"I forgot it was even in here."

"Then why won't you look at me?"

She turned and glared at him. "Satisfied?"

"Not exactly. There's more to it than that."

"What do you want me to say? That I had a horrible schoolgirl crush on you. That I kept it because you were my first love."

He grinned and took one of her hands. "Hey, that sound nice to me."

"I shouldn't have told you."

He pulled her to him. Kelsey resisted a second then came to stand between his legs. "I'm glad you did. I'm honored you thought it important enough to keep." He gave her a kiss so tender she feared she'd cry. And she'd stopped crying long ago for things that couldn't be.

CHAPTER SEVEN

JORDON WALKED BESIDE Kelsey across the neighbor's yard to look at her house. Unfortunately, the bright morning sun didn't improve the view. They stood not saying a word. Kelsey made a step forward and Jordon stopped her with a hand on her elbow.

"I'm not letting you go in there. If I could have seen this clearly I wouldn't have allowed it then."

She pulled away. "What did I say about telling me what to do?"

"I heard you. But this is a safety issue. I wouldn't let anyone enter."

Standing side by side, they looked at the house for a few more minutes.

"We need to go if we're going to make visiting hours in the ICU," Jordon said.

Kelsey nodded. Catching a glimpse of her face, he saw moisture in her eyes. He put an arm across her shoulders and pulled her to him as they made their way to his SUV.

Kelsey had a forlorn look on her face as she peered out the window as he drove.

"It's hard to believe that today can be so beautiful after yesterday."

"It is." He didn't know what else to say. He'd never seen her so down. She was always the one encouraging people, the peppy upbeat person with a quick, smart-aleck come-back. It saddened him to see her so despondent.

The floodwaters had ebbed away. Limbs and debris lay in yards and along the road. Even the trees that had fallen over the road had been cut up, and piled to the side. Along Main Street people were already out cleaning in front of their businesses, some opening early so that people could buy supplies needed for repairs. It would merely take a few days the effects of the storm would have disappeared from sight. Though the damage would linger in the hearts and minds of the residents for a long time to come, adding to the fear that it might be worse the next time.

"You know you can stay with me as long as you wish," Jordon said, hoping to draw her out of her gloom.

"I can't do that."

"Why not? Where're you going to find a place to stay for the short time you think you will be here?"

"I don't know but I'll find a place."

He wanted to protect her, reassure her and to his won-derment keep her close.

Last night had taken their relationship to a deeper level. He hated deception. Knew what it had done to him and his father, but he couldn't break his promise to Chad. Keeping his word meant everything to him. It was the foundation of trust. When he'd moved back to Golden Shores it had been to find that foundation again. The more he became involved with Kelsey, the more she shook that.

He would never have dreamed that she'd kept a nothing trinket he'd given to her so many years ago. What was he being pulled into?

It hadn't escaped his notice that Kelsey placed impor-tance on the jewelry box. She didn't strike him as senti-mental but she'd insisted that she get it when she given nothing else a second glance in the house. She'd not give that much interest to her parents' house when they'd passed it. What she had in the box was of value to her and one of those items had been the ring he'd given her.

This time, to his amazement, she did look at her parents' home when they passed. There were a few limbs in the yard, otherwise nothing was different at the neat yard and house. Was she thinking about the past, like he was?

Kelsey stood beside Jordon as they rode the elevator up to the second floor. His strong, sturdy presence had been a blessing during the fight to get Molly to the hospital, with her sorrow over her home and during the uncertain moments the night before. He'd made her forget it all with his tender but powerful lovemaking.

There had been something far too disconcerting about sharing Jordon's room as they'd dressed that morning. But nice nonetheless. She'd had Molly as support for so many years but it was comforting to have someone strong in her corner for a change. China had been there but Kelsey had hated to unload on her. She had a new husband and a baby coming, and she didn't need to carry Kelsey's burdens also. China had such a soft heart she couldn't help but morph into big-sister mode and try to fix things for her.

Squaring her shoulders and taking a deep breath, she prepared to see Molly. She and Jordon exited the elevator. When Kelsey would have stopped at the door of ICU to use the phone to ask permission to enter, Jordon pushed the door open instead. She'd forgotten he had access to almost any area of the hospital. They walked to the bed located in a corner of the large open space. Kelsey moaned when she saw Molly. Jordon took her hand and squeezed it.

He leaned over and whispered, "Hang in there. It isn't as bad as it looks."

Kelsey wasn't good with these types of injuries. That's why she'd become a nutritionist instead of a nurse. No blood.

Molly eyes were closed and she was hooked up to monitors. The bed was elevated but she lay motionless. Red angry scratches parted her pale skin. In a couple of places fine black stitches marred her appearance. Kelsey wanted to sob. Molly was so particular about caring for her skin, having her make-up on just right.

Kelsey stepped to the bedside and took one of Molly's hands. Its warmth reassured Kelsey. "Hey, there."

Molly didn't respond but Kelsey continued to talk to her. She did glance around once when the sound of two male voices caught her attention. Jordon was speaking to the surgeon who had taken care of Molly. A few minutes later Jordon came to stand beside Kelsey.

"Rick says she's doing well. They're backing off on the meds so she should be awake by this afternoon. If she's doing well by then, they'll move her out to the floor, maybe tomorrow."

Some of the pressure in her chest eased. "That sounds wonderful."

"It's almost shift-change. Why don't we go get some breakfast in the cafeteria?"

"Okay. I'll come back later."

Kelsey let Jordon escort her out of the ICU.

"I think I'll pass on food. I'm sure I have hundreds of emails to answer. I also want to check in on Mr. and Mrs. Lingerfelt if they're still here."

"They are. I asked about them when I called. And you need to eat. You've not had anything since yesterday morning. If you're not careful, you'll be sick too."

"I can take care of myself."

"I'm not saying you can't. Even if you aren't hungry, the least you could do is keep me company."

"I think you're trying to send me on a guilt trip."

He grinned. "Is it working?"

"A little bit."

"Enough to get you to share bacon and eggs with me?"

She made a resigned huff. "If I do, can I then go to my office? I need to call the landlord and my insurance company. I've got to figure out how to salvage what I can of our stuff."

Jordon looked at his watch. "It's early yet. You've got time to eat and then start on those calls."

She was hungry and she found she rather liked sharing her meals with Jordon. "Okay. I give up."

"Good. Let's go. I'm starving."

By the middle of the morning, Kelsey had answered her emails, attended a meeting for new diabetic patients where no one showed up, which was understandable, and gone up to check on Molly. Her doctor was in the process of examining her so Kelsey wasn't allowed into the ICU. She did get to speak to Molly's parents, who assured Kelsey Molly was improving.

Kelsey had phoned her landlord, who was sending his insurance representative out to look at the house. His concern had sounded genuine. She'd asked about getting her belongings and had been told she'd have to wait until the insurance people gave the okay. That hadn't improved her spirits.

She'd also checked in with China. They were supposed to have lunch the next day but decided to wait. Instead, China had invited her to dinner at her and Payton's house. She didn't tell China about the tree, not wanting her to worry.

"I don't know. Won't that be too much work for you?"

"Come on, Kelsey. I want to show you what I'm thinking about using in the baby's room."

"That's so not fair. You knew that would get me."

"Yeah, I thought it might. Why don't you bring Jordon too? He seemed to be a nice guy and he's new to town. He might like a home-cooked meal."

"That's China. Mothering everyone. Hey, you're not doing the cooking, are you?"

"No, Payton will. Part of our marriage vows were that he cooks, I help."

Kelsey laughed. "I'll think about asking Jordon and let you know."

"I'll expect you both Sunday night, six o'clock."

How like China to give her no choice. "Just because you're my big sister doesn't mean you get to tell me what to do." A few short months ago China being high-handed would have been cause for Kelsey to hang up. Now somehow it felt good to know her sister was in her corner.

"What're big sisters for? I miss you. Come on, say you'll be here."

"Okay."

"And bring Jordon?"

"I'll ask him, that's all I can do. But no matchmaking between Jordon and me, do you understand?"

"I don't have to matchmake. I saw the way he looked at you the other day. The job is already done. Bye." There was click on the line.

How like China not to give her a chance to refute that statement. Did Jordon's feelings for her go further than being his bed partner? Had things between them already gone too far?

Jordon went looking for Kelsey around five o'clock that afternoon. He'd been so busy with the new patients admitted during the storm he'd not had a chance to check on her. But she had been on his mind. Other than his ex-partner and girlfriend before the FBI had become involved, he'd never given another woman as much thought or concern as he did Kelsey.

She wasn't in her office and he was pretty sure where he'd find her. Pushing through the doors of ICU, he saw her sitting beside Molly's bed. Her eyes were still closed but she lay in a more natural position, as if she had woken up some time. An older couple sat on the other side of the bed from Kelsey.

As he approached the man rose and Kelsey did also. "Mr. Marks," she said quietly, "this is Dr. Jordon King, the man I was telling you about."

Mr. Marks put out his hand. "I understand that we…" he glanced toward the woman beside him "…owe you a large thanks for saving our daughter."

"Not at all. It was a team effort. Kelsey more than did her part."

"Either way, we're grateful."

"So how is Molly doing?" Jordon asked.

"She was awake a few minutes ago and knew who we were. Even got on to Kelsey for coming into the house to get her," Mr. Marks said.

"I'm glad to hear it."

"They plan to move her to the floor tonight," Kelsey added.

"That sounds like she is improving." Jordon looked at Kelsey. "May I speak to you a minute?"

She nodded and they stepped away from Molly's area.

Jordon said, "I wanted to let you know that I'm headed home. Do you want to ride with me? I'm in no rush."

"I've got my own car. I'll see you in a little while."

"I'm not leaving until you do because I think you'll be right here in the morning if I don't see that you go home."

"Jordon, I don't need a keeper."

"No, you don't but you do need someone to remind you to take care of yourself. Why don't you page me when you're ready to go?"

With a huff, she said, "I'm ready now. Let me say good-bye to Molly's parents."

Jordon watched as she walked over and gave first Molly's mother then her father a hug. "I'll see y'all and Molly in the morning. Let me know if anything changes."

Molly's parents assured her that they would.

Kelsey walked beside him through the ICU doors. He wanted to touch her badly, something as simple as hold her hand, but she wouldn't like that. It would be too personal. Would imply more than they were both willing to admit. He'd learned she was anti-involvement. Get too close, act like you cared too much and she'd start pushing away. This time he wasn't going to let her.

Last night had meant something to him and he refused to let her run from him now. "I'm worn out. You have to be also," he said casually.

"Yeah, but I still have to find a place to stay tonight."

Jordon stopped in the middle of the hall and glared at her.

Kelsey pursed her lips questioningly. "You're glaring at me again."

"I should be. I thought we'd talked about this already and that you would stay at my place."

She looked up and down the hallway. "This isn't the place to talk about this."

He followed suit, seeing no one. "Maybe not, but we're going to."

In a low voice Kelsey hissed, "Look, just because we

had one night of mad, passionate sex doesn't mean we're going to start living together."

"I would agree to your description of the sex and normally the moving-in part, but where else are you planning to go? You've already said it wouldn't be your parents' or sister's place."

Both were out of the question.

"Hotel?"

She didn't have that kind of money. What she did have she needed to use to set up in Atlanta.

"At least at my house you can keep an eye on what is being done at yours."

He had a point.

"You've said more than once you're leaving town soon so neither of us should be inconvenienced long."

Did he consider her an inconvenience? That idea kind of hurt. "I'll only agree if I take the sofa. You're too big for it. You looked like a sardine in a can curled up on it. And the minute I find another place there will be no argument about me leaving. Understood?"

"Something tells me that having you for a roommate isn't going to be easy. I'll most likely be glad to see you go."

Kelsey flinched. Her father had pretty much said the same thing when she'd moved out of her parents' home. She was afraid she was going to miss living with Jordon far more than she'd ever missed anything. He was beginning to fill that spot that had been empty since he and Chad had left town.

He placed a hand at her waist and gave her a slight nudge. "Come on. I'm starving for a fat, juicy burger. We can stop by the Beach Hut for some takeout and head home. I owe Hardy some attention after the last two days."

Less than an hour later she pulled her car up behind

Jordon's SUV. He got out, carrying a white sack. As she got out of her own car he called, "Hey, can you get the drinks?"

Pulling her purse up on her shoulder, Kelsey reached into his SUV and took the two soft drink cups out of the holders. Using her hip, she closed the door.

They walked to the house and Jordon unlocked the door. Once inside Kelsey placed the drinks on the counter. "Before I eat I want to go over to the house. I think I saw my landlords' car."

"Give me a sec and I'll walk with you."

"No. Stay here. I'll be back in a few minutes. Eat your burgers before they get cold." She started out the door. Jordon was beginning to encroach on her life too much.

"Are you trying to get rid of me?"

She turned back and looked at him. "If I was?"

His gaze didn't waver. "Not going to happen. If you're not back in fifteen minutes I'm coming to look for you, and I'd better not find you inside that death trap."

"Yes, sir," she snapped, but with a grin on her face. For once she didn't feel dominated by being told what to do. Jordon was concerned for her well-being. To her surprise, she rather liked being protected.

What would it be like to have that feeling all the time?

When Kelsey returned to Jordon's, he was sitting in a recliner with his feet propped up and his eyes closed. The TV was tuned to a sports channel.

Kelsey closed the door, making a low click. The burger bag sat on the counter next to the drinks, unopened. He'd not eaten without her. Her father wouldn't have thought twice about having a meal without waiting.

She'd take a shower and let him sleep. Pulling off her shoes so they wouldn't make any noise, she walked down the hall to his bedroom. Gathering her clothes and toiletries, she came back up the hall to the small second bath.

She placed her things on the counter. If she was going to have to stay here, she might well make the small place her own.

After a hot shower, she pulled on an extra-large T-shirt with a blue umbrella on it that almost covered the entire shirt and some black leggings that went to midcalf. She mussed her hair, encouraging it to dry standing up every which way.

Kelsey looked into the mirror. There were dark rings under her eyes. Sleep had been scarce over the last few days. She'd read somewhere that emotional upheaval wasn't good for your complexion. Goodness knew, she'd lived through mayhem. First Molly, then her house, then spending the night with Jordon, and now staying at his house indefinitely. Much more and she would qualify for the funny farm.

Leaning her head against the mirror, she groaned. When had her life spun so out of control? She needed the woman in Personnel in Atlanta to call before she got in too deep with Jordon.

Two quick raps to the door made her jerk straight up.

"Hey, supper is on the table when you're ready," Jordon called.

"Be there in a minute."

Even the sound of his voice through a door made her stomach flutter. She had never reacted to a guy that way before. Though that wasn't true. She'd felt the same way about Jordon when she'd been a kid.

Waiting a minute, she opened the door and headed toward the kitchen. Jordon stood with his hip against the counter and one foot crossed over the other, watching the TV and drinking through a straw. He'd changed and now wore a snug-fitting T-shirt that clung to his well-developed chest. Well-worn jeans with a straight hole at one knee rode low on his hips. All things considered, he was the sexist man she'd ever laid eyes on. Her mouth watered.

"What team do you pull for?"

He put his drink down. "I'm a Washington Redskins fan. Can't live around Washington and not become one. I thought we'd sit outside. Give Hardy a chance to run while we eat. I'll get the burgers and you carry the drinks."

"Sure."

She watched as he pulled their burgers, still in the foil wrap, out of the oven. He put them on a plate. Picking up the drinks, she led the way to the sliding glass door that faced the bay.

"I'll get the door." He came up beside her close enough that his familiar scent filled her nostrils. She was in so much trouble. Jordon pulled the door open and stepped out. There was a small round table with two chairs sitting on the cement patio.

Kelsey took one seat and he the other. The sun was still above the horizon but the sky was fast turning pink in the west.

"When I get someplace permanent I'm making sure that it has the porch facing west so I can watch the sun set every night. Even better, a sleep porch. You know, the ones with a swing bed."

"That sounds kind of kinky."

Jordon's gaze met hers and he had a quirky lift to one corner of his mouth. "Maybe you could come over and try it out with me."

"I'll be in Atlanta."

Jordon chose not respond to that remark. Kelsey seemed to use leaving as a defense mechanism and he plain wanted to forget it might happen.

"Did you talk to your landlord?" He took a bite of his food.

"Yeah. The insurance company doesn't want anyone in the house. The damage is bad enough that the house will have to be demolished."

He reached across the table and took her hand. "I'm sorry."

"Molly is the one I feel sorry for. She's in the hospital and has lost everything. It's so unfair."

"What about you? You've lost everything."

"I got the thing that truly matter the other night."

"Your box."

"Yes."

They were both quiet for a few minutes as they ate.

"Did your sister have any damage at her house?"

"They seemed to have weathered the storm pretty well. She said they lost a couple of hanging plants that they couldn't take inside because they were working at the clinic."

"I'm glad that was the worst of it."

"I haven't told her about the tree. I didn't want her hurrying over here to take care of me. We were supposed to meet for lunch this week but canceled so instead she invited me to dinner Sunday night. She wanted me to ask you to come also."

"So, are you inviting me to go to your sister's for dinner?" He grinned.

"Yes, and you don't have to make a big deal out of it."

He leaned back, stretched his legs and crossed them at the ankles. "I'm not making a big deal out of it. I'm honored."

How did the man always know the right thing to say?

They'd finished their burgers when Hardy rose from where he lay at Jordon's feet. "You ready to play, boy?"

The dog ran in a circle then picked up his stick, which was lying near him.

Kelsey laughed. "It looks like he is." It was the first real laugh she'd had in a couple of days. It felt good.

"While I clean up here, would you mind taking Hardy down to the water and playing a little fetch?" Jordon piled the leftover paper and cups on the plate.

"I can clean up."

"We'll take turns. Tomorrow night will be yours."

That was nothing like it had been growing up. Her father would never have thought of helping in the kitchen. Her mother wouldn't have thought to even ask him to. Jordon was different than any other man she knew.

"Agreed." She stood and started toward the bay.

Hardy ran ahead then turned and came back to her. When they reached the dock he raced to the end. Kelsey followed. She threw the stick into the water and in a flash Hardy was swimming after it.

Kelsey was sitting on the pier, dangling her feet over the water, when Jordon joined her.

"I left you the chair," she said, glancing at him. He had evening shadow along his jaw, which gave him a bit of a bad-boy look. She wanted to run her hand along his face to feel the prickliness. Instead, she gripped the edge of the rough wood beneath her.

"You made a beautiful picture out here. I wished I was enough of photographer to do you justice."

She narrowed her eyes at him. "That was a smooth line, Doctor."

He moved his face in close, his nose touching hers. "I'll have you know that I don't have to use lines."

"Ooh, such confidence."

He leaned back and shrugged as if he was well aware of his masculine appeal.

Kelsey looked out over the bay. The slight breeze made the water ripple. Pink, orange and yellow reflected off the water in a half circle. Her attention turned to the place she'd called home for the last three years. It looked perfect across the front but was a mangled mass from the back. Even the beautiful tree that had shaded the place for what seemed like forever was gone. It lay half in and half out of the house.

"Hey, don't be looking over there." Jordon took her hand.

"I can't help it."

Hardy returned with his stick and this time Jordon threw it, without letting go of her hand.

"Tell me about your mother."

The second she mentioned his mother he let go of her hand. Jordon didn't look her way. He seemed to focus on Hardy swimming to his stick.

"Why do you want to know about her?"

"I guess I'm curious because you don't want to talk about her," she said softly.

"There's no big mystery. Her name is Margaret and she lives in Arizona with her new husband." His tone was as flat as the now-still water.

"New? You say the word like you don't like him."

"I don't know him. Can't even tell you what he looks like." His focus still remained on Hardy.

"You've never met him?"

"Don't want to."

She turned toward him. "Why not?"

After some time he looked away from the dog and said in a hard tone, "You're not going to let it go, are you?"

"No."

Hardy returned to them, shook himself and settled behind them.

"Since you're determined to know everything then I'll tell you," he said in a harsh voice. "My mother was having an affair and I found out. I knew before my father did. I heard her talking on the phone with the man who's her new husband."

She hadn't expected that or she might not have pushed. She reached for his hand but he wouldn't allow her to take it. "Oh, Jordon, that's a horrible burden to carry."

"Yeah, it was. I didn't know whether or not to tell my dad or tell my mother that I knew. For over six months I kept it to myself. I wanted to forget. I started skipping classes, started hanging out with a different crowd."

"Chad."

"Yes, he was part of the crowd."

"After a call from one of my teachers my mother asked me what was going on. I told her that I didn't see why I had to follow the rules and do the right thing when she didn't. I could tell by the look on her face she knew what I was talking about. I explained about the phone call. That night, when Dad came home, she told him she wanted a divorce. Dad was devastated. He never said it but I think he'd guessed about the affair. He loved her so much he'd kept hoping it wasn't true. Mother left the next day. I often wondered if they'd still be together if I'd kept my mouth shut."

Kelsey took his hand between both of hers, not letting him avoid it this time. She waited until he looked at her. "That had nothing to do with you. It was between your parents."

He ran his fingers between hers and held hers on top of his thigh. "I know that now. But it took me years to place the blame where it belonged. On her."

"So that's why you don't see her."

"Yes."

"So how long has it been?" She didn't see her parents

regularly but she did keep up with them through China. She also saw them occasionally in town, driving by or in the grocery store.

"Ten years maybe. She calls on my birthday every year. Sends a present at Christmas."

She'd thought her relationship with her parents was cold. Jordon's with his mother was at subzero. "And your dad? Do you see him often?"

"Dad is great. I'll always be grateful to him for getting me straightened out. Even when he was hurting so deeply, he saw about me. He made changes in his life because he loved me and I mattered to him."

"Unlike your mother."

"Yeah. Hey, Dad is coming down next month for a visit. I want him to meet you."

Ho, that sounded like something too close to a meet-the-parents moment in a real relationship. Still, she liked the idea of meeting Jordon's father. "I'd like that, but I may be in Atlanta by then."

"Would it be so bad to stay here?"

She tugged at her hand but Jordon wouldn't release it. "Please, don't start. I've been working and dreaming for years of moving to a bigger city. This is my chance and I'd appreciate you not making it harder."

He was quiet for a moment. "I promise not to mention it again."

They sat in peace until the last ray of the sun had been swallowed up by darkness. Jordon released her hand and stood, then helped her up. He wrapped an arm around her waist and pulled her close as they walked back to the house. He pushed back the sliding screen and let Kelsey enter first. Hardy squeezed past her.

"Hardy, you're not much of a gentleman," Jordon said, as he closed the glass door.

Kelsey laughed, something she seemed to do more when she was around Jordon. She like to laugh. In fact, sitting on the pier, watching the sunset and talking had been one of the nicest things she'd done in a long time. Despite all the turmoil in her life, Jordon seemed like a safe spot in the storm.

"You want something to drink? Watch some TV?"

"You don't have to treat me like I'm a guest."

"Tonight I've decided you are a guest. Tomorrow you can clean the bathrooms. I hate cleaning bathrooms."

She smirked. "You do know how to make a roommate feel at home."

His chuckle warmed her from the inside out.

"So what about that drink?"

"I don't think so. But I wouldn't mind watching some TV."

"The remote is over by the recliner. Pick out whatever you like except a home-decorating show."

"That sounded a little chauvinistic."

"I'm not. I just don't get into that stuff."

She picked up the remote and turned on the TV. Flipping through the channels, she said, "I like those decorating shows. I'd love to have a place of my own to decorate. I've never lived where I could make a place my own." She stopped at a crime drama. "Hey, I love this show."

"That's one of my favorites too."

Kelsey took a seat on the sofa and curled her legs under her. Jordon didn't join her. Instead, he took the recliner. A tickle of disappointment went through her that he didn't sit beside her. They spent the next hour watching the show and talking about what had happened over the season and where they thought the show was going during the commercial.

After the show, Jordon put the footrest on the recliner

down and stood. "I've got an early morning so I'm going to call it a night. I'll get you some sheets and a blanket."

Well, at least he was going to follow her rules without an argument.

He returned with an armload of bed linen. "I was going to tell you to make yourself at home in the spare bath but I can see you've done that already. Tomorrow evening I'll move some things around in the closet in my office and you can hang your clothes there."

She took the items from his arms. "Thanks. You have been great and I appreciate it."

"It's the least I can do for a neighbor."

Last night she had been his lover and now she was only his neighbor.

She was tucking the sheet in around the cushions of the sofa when Jordon said, "Kelsey."

"Uh." When he said nothing more she looked at him.

"I want you to know I'd like to have you in my bed next to me more than anything. Don't think that because I don't ask, it's not what I want. I'll respect your requests but know all you have to do is walk down the hall. Rest well, Kelsey."

She watched Jordon's broad back as he headed for his bedroom. Yeah, right. After that speech he thought she'd rest well? He left the door wide open, as if to say he was there if she wanted him.

Kelsey shoved down the desire to go after him and throw her arms around his neck. That wouldn't help her keep her heart from breaking when she had to leave. She picked up the blanket and gave it a sharp shake, opening it.

Going to the bathroom, she washed her face and brushed her teeth. The water was running on the other side of the wall as well. Jordon must be taking a shower. Water would be rolling over his handsome face, across his chest, down his muscled thighs.

Kelsey put her toothbrush down and all but ran back to the sofa. She crawled under the sheet and blanket and pulled them both up to her neck. Tomorrow she'd start looking for another place to stay.

She tried not to listen as he pulled out a drawer, pushed it back, the squeak of the bed as he lay down, and the click of the light switch before the house was washed in darkness.

Each tick of the clock sounded like a gong as she forced herself to sleep. If she slept she couldn't think about the warm, hard body that would curl around her if she went to him or the tender kisses Jordon would place along the curve of her ear. Worse, the feel of his lips on her breasts that would cause her to throb and tremble with need.

Jordon wanted her. Had said it. Shown it. She wanted him. That was the real problem. She was desperate for him. So why was she fighting it? Because she'd have a devil of a time leaving him behind. Still, a short time with Jordon was better than no time.

Kelsey threw the covers back. She was going to spend every night in Jordon's arms that she could. Padding down the hall, she paused at the door for a second before going to stand beside the bed.

Suddenly a hand grabbed her wrist and jerked her downward. She yelped seconds before she came in contact with the warm skin of Jordon's chest.

"It's about damn time you showed up," he growled, before his mouth took hers.

CHAPTER EIGHT

SUNDAY DAWNED A bright warm fall day on the coast. Jordon declared his life better for his move back to Golden Shores. He and Kelsey had slept in and together cooked a huge breakfast. Now they sat on the pier. He in the chair and her on his lap, Hardy beside them.

Since the night she'd come to him, Kelsey hadn't backed away once. One morning she'd even allowed him to kiss her goodbye when he'd walked her to her office. He'd like to have a chance to do that always. He felt good about himself around Kelsey, as if life was a rich playground and she was his playmate. If he could only convince her to stay in Golden Shores just a little bit longer, but that was a subject he'd promised not to bring up and one he didn't want to talk about anyway.

"Hey, what time are we supposed to be at your sister's?"

"Around six."

"Great. I'll have time to see the game. The Redskins play today."

"So I'm going to be a football widow?"

"Don't sound so pitiful. I'll let you watch it with me."

She sat up so he could see her eyes. "Why, that's mighty big of you."

"I thought so. Come on." He pushed on her butt, nudging her off his lap. "We don't want to miss the kickoff."

"Ooh, I can hardly wait." She wiggled all over.

Jordon hugged her close until she giggled. "You're such a funny woman."

Thirty minutes later Jordon looked at Kelsey in disbelief and admiration. She could carry on an intelligent conversation about football, even knowing the names of a number of men on the Redskins' team. Kelsey was a woman after his own heart. In fact, he was afraid that she might already have it.

At halftime he said, "Want some popcorn?"

"Sure. I've not had any in a long time."

Jordon found a boiler, placed it on the stove then added oil. He was looking through the cabinet when Kelsey asked, "What're you doing?"

"I'm looking for the popcorn."

"No, I mean with the boiler."

"That's how I cook popcorn. The old-fashioned way."

"I've never seen it popped like this before. Microwave is the way I go."

"My grandmother made it this way, so did my mother and now I do."

"I know you don't like to talk about your mother but this isn't the first time you've mentioned her when you were doing something."

There was some truth to that statement. As much as he wanted to believe his mother meant nothing in his life, she still influenced him. He poured the corn into the boiler. "I guess she was a good mother at one time."

"We all can't be perfect all the time."

By the time the game started again they were seated on the sofa, munching on popcorn with soft drinks in glasses nearby. Kelsey yawned widely at the beginning of the third quarter, mumbled a comment about someone keeping her up all night, laid her head on his thigh and seconds later was asleep.

Jordon pulled down the blanket that stayed on the back of the sofa and covered her. He rested a hand at her waist. What a perfect way to spend a Sunday afternoon—the Redskins on TV and Kelsey close. What would it take to make this happen all the time?

He had to see Chad and remove the proverbial elephant from between them if he wanted any kind of future with Kelsey. Jordon didn't look forward to telling her. The scene would be ugly. Still, it had to be done. It was long overdue. If he waited any longer it would be worse. Maybe with that part of her life truly behind Kelsey he could convince her they belonged together. That staying in Golden Shores with him was worth the risk.

At five minutes to six Kelsey said, "Make a right into the drive of that yellow house. It's China and Payton's."

"Nice place." Jordon followed Kelsey up the long stairs. "I've got to start looking for a place before my lease is up. I've put off doing anything about it because I'm not good with the details. Like are there enough bathrooms. Would you go house-hunting with me some time this week?"

It sounded too permanent. Like something a couple did together. "I don't know."

"Kelsey, I could really use your opinion."

She would enjoy seeing inside homes and looking at how they were decorated. Having a chance to imagine what she would do with one if it was hers. "I guess I could, if you really want me to."

"Of course I do. Having someone along to help would at least get me moving in the right direction. Do you think you could take off on Tuesday afternoon if I can get a real estate person to set some places up?"

"I guess. I have time coming for the other night during the storm."

"Good. Then it's a date."

Kelsey smiled. She'd had to look at three places in town to find a hot pink bikini this late in the season. She'd carried it to Molly who had been moved to a room two days earlier. Kelsey had broken the bad news about the house and Molly had seemed to take it well, just relieved to be alive. Kelsey had dangled the bag with the bikini in it off the end of her index finger.

"What's in that?"

"Your winnings."

"Winnings?"

"Yeah, you won the bet about who the new doctor would date."

Molly had squealed, then winced. "So he asked you out?"

"Well, not exactly." Kelsey had smiled and drawn the last word out.

Molly had given her a quizzical look then her eyes had widened and her mouth had formed an O. "You've been to bed with him!"

"Hey, what're you thinking? You have a huge smile on your face," Jordon said, bringing her back to the present as they waited on someone to answer China and Payton's door.

"I was just thinking about Molly's reaction to winning a bet."

"You mean the one about who I would ask out first?"

She stepped back and looked at him with narrowed eyes. "Who told you?"

"No one really. I kind of figured it out."

"Why didn't you say something?"

He grinned and said in a low voice, "It didn't matter.

You've been my pick since you asked me to dance the night we met."

"Why, that's one of the nicest compliments I've ever received." She went up on her toes and kissed him.

She broke the kiss to find China standing in the open doorway, looking from her to Jordon and back again with a grin on her face. "Well, I was going to say come in but if you'd rather wait awhile I'll understand."

Kelsey stepped away from Jordon and beamed at China. Jordon's hand remained at her waist. "No, we're ready to come in."

China opened the door wider. "Welcome."

"Thanks for inviting me to dinner," Jordon said as he stepped into the house.

"Payton will be glad to have another male around while Kelsey and I chat." She pointed to the right and through the living room. "He's in the kitchen, finishing up the meal and watching the football game. Why don't you go in and keep him company? I'm going to show Kelsey's the baby's room."

Kelsey watched Jordon walk away with a knowing grin on his face then she turned to her sister. "That wasn't remotely subtle."

"I had no intention of it being subtle. Come on, I'll show you where we plan to put the baby then you can spill."

Should she tell China that Jordon had been Chad's friend? That wasn't a secret she should be keeping.

China led her down the hall and into the small room across from the master bedroom. The second they stepped into the room China turned and faced Kelsey with an eager look on her face. "Okay, tell all."

"There's not much to say." She made a point of looking out a window at the ocean.

"Oh, come on, Kelsey. I thought we were trying to be

sisters like we once were. You used to share everything with me."

Kelsey decided she might as well tell China what had been happening between her and Jordon. She would badger her until she did. Even when they had rarely seen each other China hadn't given up on her. Kelsey faced her. "He's from the Washington area. He's a doctor—"

China put her hands on her hips. "That's not what I'm talking about and you know it! Start with that hot kiss on my porch."

"He moved in two doors down. A tree went through mine and Molly's house during the storm. Molly was trapped and Jordon saved her life."

"What? Why I'm I just hearing about this now? Were you at home when it happened?"

"No, I was working at the hospital. I'm on Jordon's team and he saw that I was worried. We went in search of Molly."

"How is she?"

"She's doing well but still in the hospital."

"Good," China said, relief in her voice. "But we're getting sidetracked. I want to know about *you* and Jordon."

"My house was condemned and he's letting me stay at his house." Warmth filled her cheeks. "One thing led to another…"

China raised her brows. "It did, did it?"

Kelsey looked away. "Yeah."

"I knew there was something going on between the two of you at the picnic. You really like him, don't you?"

"I do. More every day."

"So-o-o, are you planning to stay around here after all?"

The eagerness in China's voice made Kelsey wince and her heart constrict. She truly sounded like she wanted

Kelsey to remain close. "No, I'm still planning to take the job in Atlanta if they want me."

"I had hoped that Jordon might change your mind where I couldn't."

Kelsey met her gaze again. "China, there's something else I need to tell you. Jordon used to live in Golden Shores. He was Chad's friend."

China said nothing for a moment. "I told Payton that Jordon looked familiar for some reason. Now I remember." China's voice went higher. "He called himself J-man. He gave you that yellow ring you wore forever. You had such a crush on him."

"I did and I'm afraid that I still do."

China laughed. "It's about time some man got past that ten-foot-high electric fence you have built around you."

"Enough about me. Tell me what you have planned for this room."

Fifteen minutes later they joined the men in the kitchen. They were standing in front of the TV, screaming at the football game on the screen. She and China looked at each other. There was a catch in Kelsey's chest. This was what it felt like to have a happy family circle.

Before they disturbed the men, China put her hand on Kelsey's arm and stopped her. "I don't want this to ruin the evening but I have to ask, does Jordon know where Chad is, what happened to him?"

Kelsey shook her head.

China gave her a sad smile. "I guess that was too much to hope for," she said, before she put on a happy face. "Okay, men, it's time for dinner."

"Aw, honey, we're under the two-minute warning," Payton called over his shoulder.

"Okay, you're the chef. Kelsey and I will be out on the porch. Call us when you're ready."

"Will do," Payton said, already focused on the game again.

Jordon's gaze met Kelsey's and he winked, sending a tingle along her spine, before he joined Payton at the game again.

There was a momentary lull in the conversation at the dining table and China looked at Jordon. "I remember you now."

Jordon chest constricted. Was this how an animal felt when it was trapped? Had Kelsey told her about his and Chad's relationship? "I didn't recognize you at first either."

"What're y'all talking about?" Payton asked, looking from China to Jordon.

"Jordon was Chad's friend."

"Chad? Your brother."

"Yes," China said. "I wish we knew where he was." She looked a Kelsey.

Jordon shifted in his seat. Guilt washed over him. Chad's disappearance had affected China as strongly as it had Kelsey. Deception didn't appeal to him on any level. He was keeping a secret that directly affected someone he cared about and he didn't see a blameless way out. Had his mother felt the same way? Been unable to tell the truth because she'd feared the hurt she'd inflict? It didn't make what she'd done right but it did help to explain her actions.

He had to ease their suffering. Last week he'd called the prison and been told he couldn't visit for another week. When he did get to see Chad he would insist he agree to let him tell his family he was alive. He couldn't keep it from them any longer. He'd already kept the secret far too long.

Payton took China's hand. "Honey, maybe one day you'll know something."

The evening was no longer enjoyable for Jordon.

An hour later he and Kelsey said their goodbyes. Jordon drove and Kelsey leaned her head on his shoulder, placed her hand on his thigh. He laid a hand on top of hers.

Could the weight on his chest feel heavier? What he and Kelsey had was tentative at best and he held an explosive secret that could tear them apart more effectively than her moving to Atlanta. When she found out he'd been keeping knowledge of Chad from her she would never speak to him again. How had he managed to get himself in such a mess?

"You're mighty quiet," Kelsey said, her breath tickling his neck.

"I was just thinking how glad I am that you invited me to your sister's." What a liar he was. Something he detested. He was becoming his mother.

"I didn't really. It was China's idea."

Jordon glanced at her and saw her smirk.

"I'm glad you came too." She squeezed his thigh before her fingers wandered upward.

"You know, if you don't stop that I'll have to pull over. I can see it now, the policeman with his flashlight shining on your cute bare tush."

"How do you know it wouldn't be yours?"

"Either way it might be embarrassing."

She giggled. "It might at that. Knowing our luck, it'll be one of the old-timers and he'll recognize both of us."

He couldn't help but smile at that idea. "Why don't you behave and I'll drive a little faster."

Her hand moved on his leg. "Why don't you just drive faster," she cooed.

* * *

Tuesday afternoon Kelsey was finishing her last notes on a patient when Jordon stepped through the open doorway of her office. The man made her heart beat a little faster every time she saw him. It would kill her to leave him, but she would. Maybe they could work it out to see each other on weekends. Spend vacations together. Who was she kidding? After a while that would become more difficult, and soon they would grow apart. That thought made her sad.

"Hey, you okay?" Jordon asked.

He always seemed to read her so well. She'd have to start covering her emotions better around him. She plastered a smile on her face. "Yeah."

"Great. Are you ready to go house-hunting?"

"I am. Give me a sec to put these files away."

He leaned a shoulder against the door and crossed one foot over the other. "Take your time but we have to meet the agent in fifteen minutes."

"You're too funny. Have you thought about giving up your day job and going into comedy?" Kelsey asked, as she gathered up her folders and filed them in a cabinet.

"No, but I thought about becoming a professional dancer."

She turned to face him with a grin on her face. "Ooh, I wouldn't do that. I've seen you dance. You're a much better doctor."

He bowed. "Why, thank you, ma'am. I do believe that was a compliment."

"I think it was more of a statement of fact."

Jordon stepped further in the room. "You know, you can give me a compliment."

"I don't think so. It might go to your head."

Jordon's hands found her waist and pulled her close.

His lips met hers seconds before his tongue demanded entrance. He shifted, widening his stance to bring her into more intimate contact. He lifted his lips but his mouth remained a hair's breathe from hers. She moaned with need.

"There, you can compliment me."

She pushed back and he let her go. "You were playing with me."

"No, I wasn't. You looked so delicious I wanted to kiss you and if I could get a compliment from you at the same time, even better."

"What compliment?"

"That moan was a loud and clear one."

She huffed. "I did not!"

He grinned. "Would you like to ask the man in the office down the hall?"

She turned and picked up her purse. "Don't we have somewhere to be?"

Two hours and three houses later Kelsey sat beside Jordon as he pulled his SUV next to the real estate woman's car in yet another drive. This two-story home was painted a light blue and trimmed in white, with wide steps leading to a dark oak front door. The entire look was welcoming. The expansive porch had long windows that looked as if they could be opened. The yard had been beautifully landscaped with foliage along the porch and beside the handrails. Large chrysanthemums filled the urns on either side of the entrance. Kelsey let out a small sound of awe.

"Like the look of this one, do ya?"

She'd worked hard to keep her opinions to herself as they'd looked at the other houses. It had only been when Jordon had asked what she thought that she'd voiced her view of a home. Even then she was uncomfortable doing so. She shouldn't be helping him make a decision on something as important as a house. His wife should do that.

His wife. A sick feeling filled her stomach. The wife who wouldn't be her.

"Are you coming?" Jordon asked, as he opened the door.

She pasted a smile on her face and climbed out of the car. "I am."

The real estate woman unlocked the front door with a flourish. "This one you could move right into. It was only finished a couple of months ago. Unfortunately the family was transferred out of the state and never got to live here." She walked further into the large open living area. "There are five bedrooms. Plenty of space for a family. Let me show you the rest of the house."

Family? Kelsey lagged behind as the other two moved though the rooms. She ran her fingertips along the Italian tile counter in the kitchen. She might start cooking if she had a wonderful place like this one to do it in. The master bedroom and bath were larger than her and Molly's whole bungalow. What would it be like to live in this grand home, have children running around who looked like Jordon?

"Kelsey?"

"Uh?"

"I asked you what you think."

"Oh, it's nice." What she wanted to stay was that it was the most perfect house she'd ever seen.

"You still need to see the outside. You'll love it," the real estate woman fussed.

Kelsey couldn't imagine that being the case. But it was wonderful. The back of the house was similar to the front, with a large porch running the length of it with a screened-in area at one end.

Jordon leaned over and whispered, "This would be a perfect spot for a swinging bed."

The woman moved further ahead of them and down the steps into the yard. He made it sounded so cozy and sensual that Kelsey shivered. It would be heaven to spend a rainy night gently swaying in a bed with Jordon. She shook herself mentally. Those thoughts had to stop.

The real estate woman waited on the half circle slate patio at the bottom of the steps. The manicured yard lay between them and the bay beyond. There was a T-shaped pier with a white gazebo on one section of the T. Thank goodness the real estate woman's chatter covered Kelsey's quietness. This place was the home of her dreams. But it wasn't to be hers. Jordon's maybe, but never hers.

"How many acres again?" Jordon asked.

"Two point five."

Jordon looked at Kelsey. "There would be plenty of room for Hardy to run."

Kelsey nodded, looking out over the space.

The real estate woman's phone buzzed. "Do you two mind walking down to the pier without me? I need to return this call."

"Sure, that's fine," Jordon told her. He took Kelsey's hand and they strolled to the water. "It's more than I had really planned to start out with, but I like it. What do you think?"

"It's nice," Kelsey said in a flat voice.

He stopped her short of stepping onto the dock. "You don't like it?" Disbelief filled his voice.

"It's beautiful, Jordon, but it really doesn't matter if I like it or not. It will be your house. I won't be living here."

They walked to the end of the dock. "You could if you wanted to."

"I'm planning to move to Atlanta."

"So you can leave just like that?" He sounded hurt.

"I'm not leaving 'just like that'. I told you when we started this that I planned to leave."

"I know, and I agreed to keep things simple between us.

I'm sorry if I was applying pressure. I want what's best for you. If that's moving out of Golden Shores then I'll have to accept it. Maybe right now isn't the right time for me to be thinking of buying a house."

"You shouldn't let what I'm doing affect your decisions."

"There's no hurry on this house idea. Who knows, I might become so enamored with you I can't live without you and decide to move to Atlanta."

An ache filled her chest. What had she let happen? Would she want that for him? Jordon had moved back to Golden Shores to find peace and start over, and he had. Could she, would she, want to take him away from that? She smiled up and him. "Come on, let go and see the gazebo."

They were walking around the side of the house on their way back to the SUV when her cell phone this be the call she'd been waiting for?

"I need to answer this. I'll just be a minute." She stepped away from where Jordon and the real estate woman stood.

Jordon was half listening to the ongoing prattle of the real estate woman about other homes she wanted to show him. Instead, his focus was on Kelsey. He'd hardly noticed when the real estate lady had said she'd call him soon. Kelsey's face lit up. Jordon knew without asking this was the phone call from Atlanta she'd been expecting and he'd been dreading.

That was the moment he knew. He'd fallen hopelessly in love with Kelsey and he was destined for the same heartache as his father. Even if he could convince Kelsey to stay or if he moved with her, the issue of Chad would still tear them apart. Their days were numbered.

She'd finished her conversation and was now coming

toward him with a bright smile on her face. He made an effort to match it. "Hey, is everything all right?"

"Better than all right. They want me in Atlanta on Friday for an interview."

His world wasn't fine. It was falling apart again. It had happened when his mother had left and one more time when he'd had to give up his job in Washington. The difference was this time his heart was involved and it would be far more devastating.

"But if you care for someone you support them, want the best for them, and you let them go." That's what his father had said when he had asked why he hadn't fought for his mother to stay. His father had cared so much that he'd put her happiness above his own.

Jordon put his arm around Kelsey's shoulders and squeezed her to him. "That's wonderful, honey."

She gave him a narrow-eyed look. "I didn't think you'd be happy."

"If this is what you think you need to do then I think you need to go. I want what's best for you."

Kelsey wrapped her arms around his waist and hugged him. "That means a lot to me. I've spent years with a father who micromanaged everything I did and most times told me what to do. So I appreciate the support."

Jordon was thankful for his father's wisdom that was now serving him well. He only hoped he could remember it as he watched Kelsey leave for Atlanta that final time.

CHAPTER NINE

THURSDAY AFTERNOON KELSEY was paged to the second-floor heart wing. She walked up to the nursing desk. "Someone need me?"

A woman who Kelsey had known since high school said, "Yes. Dr. King. He's in Room 207."

"Thanks."

"Hey, Kelsey." She turned to look back at the nurse. "You know we're all jealous. He's a keeper."

Kelsey couldn't deny the feeling of pride that filled her. "Yeah, I know."

At the door of the room Kelsey knocked then pushed it open. She heard the soft sound of Spanish being spoken by a female and the return of a deeper voice in the same language. To her surprise there was a middle-aged, dark-skinned man in the bed, a woman standing beside it and Jordon. The patient was hooked up to monitors but otherwise looked fine. All too well, Kelsey knew that was the case for most heart patients.

The woman spoke and Jordon answered. Kelsey had had no idea he spoke fluent Spanish. The man continued to surprise her. Since his initial response to her going to Atlanta he'd made only encouraging remarks. Their love-making had been nothing short of phenomenal. Anna, the nurse, was right. He was a keeper. So why was she so willing to leave him? She wasn't but getting a job in a city and moving away from Golden Shores had been her dream forever. What if she stayed to be with him and he left? He'd done that years ago. He'd not said anything about making their relationship permanent. If he did, would she agree?

"Ms. Davis," Jordon said, looking her direction. "This is Mr. and Mrs. Sanchez. They are from Colombia. Mr. Sanchez has had a mild heart attack. We're going to keep him here for a few days for monitoring." Jordon paused and translated what he'd said then looked at Kelsey again. "I would like you to work with him on his diet while he's here." He spoke to the couple and they nodded.

Kelsey smiled at the man and woman. "Nice to meet you. I'll be glad to help." She looked at Jordon. "May I see you in the hall for a moment, Dr. King?"

He spoke to the couple and then followed her out into the hall. "Is there a problem?"

"Here's a big one. I don't speak Spanish and the translator is out sick today."

Jordon seemed to think then he said, "I'll do the translating. You do have your handouts in Spanish, don't you?"

"Of course."

"Good. Can you meet me here in an hour? That should give me enough time to find someone to cover for me for a while."

"I'll be here. What's the urgency?"

"I'm just afraid that Mr. Sanchez might not stay long enough to hear this if we don't do it right away."

"If that's the case, do you think he'll pay attention to what we say?"

"No, but I think his wife will and she'll see that he follows it."

"You are a smart man, Dr. King."

He grinned. "I like to think so but it is always nice to hear it from you."

She jutted her jaw. "See, I *can* give an unsolicited compliment."

"You can and I shall reward you for it later this evening." He gave her a wolfish look that made heat rush to places it shouldn't when she was at work.

"I'll see you in an hour."

Jordon was taking to Anna at the nurses' station when she returned to the floor. Another young nurse hovered nearby. Every once in a while she would glance at Jordon as if she'd like to have his attention. Never before had Kelsey wanted to walk up and kiss a man in front of everyone just to prove that he was hers. She'd never cared enough before for it to matter. Resisting the urge to make a public spectacle of herself, she walked up and stood by Jordon. Anna's lips curved up and the other nurse picked up a chart, gave Jordon one last glance and headed down the hall.

Jordon looked at Kelsey and smiled. The one she recognized as hers alone.

"I'm ready when you are," Kelsey said, smiling back.

"Then let's get started."

Mr. and Mrs. Sanchez greeted them as she and Jordon entered the room. Kelsey pulled a spare chair from the corner and placed it next to the bed. "Please, ask Mrs. Sanchez to pull her chair around next to mine," she told Jordon, but smiled at Mrs. Sanchez.

He did as she requested.

"Now, I know this may be overwhelming but you can stop me any time if you have a question."

Jordon translated as Kelsey opened a notebook with Mr. Sanchez's name on the front. So it went for the next hour. When they finished Jordon looked tired and she knew she was. It had taken twice as long to explain the heart-smart diet because she had to stop and let Jordon repeat what she'd said. They managed to get through everything and the Sanchezes had even ask a few questions.

As they left the room Jordon said, "I'll be in to see you tomorrow."

Kelsey started to say the same but stopped herself. She wouldn't be here. She'd be in Atlanta. On Monday she'd check in on Mr. Sanchez if he hadn't already been discharged. She smiled and gave a slight wave before she headed toward the door. Mr. Sanchez said something. Kelsey turned and saw him taking his wife's hand. He spoke to Jordon. He smiled and looked at Kelsey and said something back to Mr. Sanchez.

"Thanks for helping out there," Jordon said, as they walked down the hall.

"Hey, I was doing my job. You were the one helping me out. Do you think he'll stay in the hospital long enough to have the test he needs?"

"I think he will now."

"Why?"

"Because of you."

"Me?"

"He told me that if everyone was as nice as you then maybe he should stay. You made the difference."

"I didn't do anything special."

"You just being you is special."

She placed her hand on his arm. He stopped and looked at her. "Thank you. That's the nicest thing anyone has said to me."

"Honey." His voice was soft with sincerity. "There's a lot of special things about you. Let's get out of here and I'll name them for you."

Jordon kept his promise. During the night he told her

something special about herself as he kissed the back of her knee, as he nuzzled the sweet spot behind her ear and just before they became one. He whispered more qualities when he woke her in the wee hours of the morning and made love to her again.

The next morning, as he drove her to the airport in Jackson, they were both quiet. Jordon had insisted that she not drive to Atlanta but fly. She complained she didn't have the money for a ticket and he wouldn't take no for an answer, insisting he buy it. She'd admitted she'd never flown before and Jordon had assured her it was a short flight and she'd be fine. After much discussion back and forth, she'd relented and let him have his way. The truth was she dreaded leaving Jordon any sooner than she had to, and flying would give her more time with him.

He pulled to the curb in front of Departures. Kelsey met him at the back of the SUV to get the small overnight bag she'd brought for the trip.

"Call me when you get to the hotel so I'll know you're safe," Jordon said.

It was nice to be worried over. That was one of the things her father had done to the extreme and she'd found she had missed that to a certain extent. "I will. You don't have to worry about me. I'm a big girl."

"I know. But when you care about someone you tend to worry."

Had that been how her father had felt?

"I'll be here waiting tomorrow evening. Just give me a call when you land and I'll pull around to get you."

"I will." She smiled at him. "After all, you're my only way home."

"You remember that and don't take off with just any man." He hugged her close for a second then gave her a tender kiss. "I'll miss you."

"I'm only going to be gone overnight."

"I know but that doesn't mean I won't miss you."

"I'll miss you too. Bye." Kelsey took the handle of her luggage and pulled the bag through the door of the airport. She had to go now or she never would. Moisture filled her eyes. If she got this job she was afraid it would tear her heart out when she left Jordon for good.

Maybe with this separation she could get some perspective. Heaven knew, she had none when he was close.

Before daylight the next day Jordon driving up the interstate on his way to the state prison. He had called ahead so Chad would know he had a visitor. Jordon had to make him understand that his family must be told where he was. If not for their sakes then for his own. Jordon couldn't keep that knowledge to himself any longer.

As promised, Kelsey had phoned when she'd arrived at her hotel room. She'd sounded excited and said the plane ride had been a wonderful experience. Jordon wished he'd had the opportunity to share that with her. To see her eyes light up with wonder. Hold her hand for reassurance when they landed. He hadn't volunteered to go with her. Seeing Chad had been more important.

She'd called him again later that evening to tell him she thought the interview had gone great. The person she'd spoken to had promised to let her know something by the beginning of the week. She'd sounded so excited that he was both thrilled for her but pained for himself. Could he let her go? He had no interest in being involved in large hospital politics again, but if that was what it took to have Kelsey in his life, he would seriously consider moving to Atlanta.

He couldn't spend another night like the night before. Tossing and turning for hours, he'd finally moved to the recliner. That hadn't been much better. Without Kelsey nothing seemed to suit.

Three hours later, Jordon faced Chad through the window of the visiting cubicle of the state penitentiary.

"Hey, bud, this is an unexpected visit. I thought you wouldn't be back for a couple of months," Chad said.

Jordon hated seeing a human being locked up but was pleased to see Chad looking well. "I know, but something has come up that I need to talk to you about."

Chad's forehead wrinkled. "What's that?"

"I've met your sisters. I came to tell you that I can no longer keep it a secret that I know you're here. I have to tell them you are alive."

Chad sat forward. "How did you meet them?"

"Kelsey and I work together at the hospital. I met her the third day I was in town. She introduced me to China at a hospital picnic."

"So what do they do?"

Chad seemed eager to know everything about his sisters, asking questions until Jordon told him all he knew.

"So China's going to be a mother," Chad said with a smile on his face. "And does Kelsey have a husband?"

For once in Jordon's life he wanted to say yes and it was him. "No, but I am hoping some time soon that I can convince her that I would make a good one."

Chad leaned back in his chair, crossed his arms over his chest and grinned. "Well, well. You have the hots for my sister."

"That, and I love her. So you can see why I need to tell her about you. China has to know. Your parents too. I didn't want to break a promise without telling you first that I was going to do it. I'm already afraid Kelsey may not speak to me again. I've kept the secret too long."

"I'm sorry I put you in that position, man. I just didn't

want my family to know that they had a jailbird for a member. I never really thought you would ever meet them. I didn't even know they still lived in Golden Shores."

"I'm going to tell Kelsey tonight or no later than tomorrow."

"Okay."

Jordon was relieved to have Chad's agreement, but he would have told Kelsey anyway. He visited a few more minutes with Chad then said goodbye. He still had to drive to Jackson to pick Kelsey up at the airport. Maybe the hours he was on the road would give him the time to configure a plan to approach the subject of Chad and keep her from hating him. He feared he could use all the drive time and more, and still not make that happen.

Kelsey stood at the curb of the airport pick-up area, shifting from one foot to the other. Despite the interview going well, she'd missed Jordon so much she'd been unhappy the entire time she'd been gone. The plane ride had been exciting but the whole time she'd been wishing Jordon had been beside her. She'd never been to a city as large as Atlanta. Overwhelmed would be an understatement of how she'd felt. Could she live there? Was this really what she wanted?

The three interviewers had been impressed by her answers. She'd seen it on their faces. She felt good about being offered the job. Would she take it if they did? Just a few short weeks ago she would have jumped at it. Now she wasn't so sure. Somewhere during that time she'd started wanting Jordon more. Her new relationship with China made Golden Shores feel more like home. With Jordon there, it might be the only place for her.

A thrill of joy ran through her as she watched the big blue SUV pull to the curb. Seconds later Jordon had her wrapped in his arms, her feet dangling above the ground.

Kelsey enfolded his neck and squeezed him as tightly as he was her.

"I missed you," he said into her hair.

"I missed you too." She had. It felt wonderful being in his arms again.

"Let's go home. I'd like to show you how much." He gave her a quick kiss on the lips then put her bag in the vehicle.

She grinned. "I think I'd like that."

Jordon couldn't bring himself to ruin the blissful reunion he and Kelsey had by talking about Chad or even asking if she would take the job if it was offered to her. As if by agreement, she didn't mention her trip outside of saying Atlanta was a huge city.

"Would you like to stop for a nice dinner?" he asked, before they left the city limits of Jackson.

"No." She placed her hand on his thigh. "I'd rather just go home."

He liked the fact she called his place home, even if she might not have meant it in the same context as he wished. "Then home it is."

Kelsey slept part of the way, as if her night hadn't been much more restful than his. Satisfaction filled him to think she might have been as lonely without him as he had been without her. Even after she woke, she didn't say much. He didn't either, just happy to have her beside him.

In Golden Shores he went through a fast-food restaurant and ordered them a takeout meal. It was dark by the time he pulled into his drive.

Inside Kelsey said, "Let me have my bag and I'll unpack."

"Are you ready to eat?"

"I'd like to get a shower and change clothes first. Go on without me." She headed down the hall.

There was a tension in the air, as if they were both circling subjects that neither wanted to talk about. She had no idea about his and he didn't want to know about hers. He wished he could turn the clock back twenty-four hours to the way it had been between them before she'd left. Once they talked, nothing would be the same. Had his mother and father felt the same way? Was that why they'd never faced their problems?

The water was no longer running and Jordon expected Kelsey to join him any minute, but instead she called, "Hey, Jordon, could you come here a minute?"

"Sure." He rose from the recliner and went down the hall. As he went through the door of the bedroom he went statue still. Kelsey stood beside the bed in a long pink satiny negligée with only the thinnest of lace covering her breasts. She was gorgeous.

His mouth went dry. His manhood rose in reaction to the sexy and desirable picture before him. He was never a man at a loss for words, but this time he could only stare.

"I bought you a present." She shifted, which made the flowing fabric move, giving him a glimpse of a long trim thigh and hot-pink painted toenails.

That proved to heat his body's reaction more. She was seducing him and he loved it.

"I saw it and thought you might like it, but..." Kelsey looked away as if insecure.

Had he ever seen Kelsey look anything but confident? He couldn't remember a time.

He stalked toward her. "Oh, honey, I love it."

She smiled then kissed him with enough passion that he couldn't remove his clothes fast enough.

Some time later, with her snuggled in his arms, he said, "Thank you for the gift. I hope you buy them for me often."

"Mmm." Seconds later she slept.

It was late afternoon the next day when he and Kelsey were walking to the dock that he blurted, "Kelsey, we need to talk."

He couldn't put it off any longer. It was eating him alive not to tell her about Chad, though he was worried sick that it might kill him when he did. He had kept a secret that had broken his father's heart and now he'd been keeping one that would break his.

She looked away for a second then met his gaze and said, "I know. I need to talk to you too."

"Let's go out on the pier."

Since there was only one chair Jordon sat on the pier and she took a place beside him but at arm's length. Kelsey let one leg dangle over the edge and brought the other into a ninety-degree angle onto the boards to face him. Hardy left them to sniff around the edge of the water.

"Kelsey, I need to tell you something. I don't know a good way to do this so I'm just going to say it."

She gave him probing look.

"Chad is alive."

She leaned toward him, her eyes wide. "How do you know?"

"I've seen him."

"Where?"

"He's in the state prison about three hours from here, doing five years for drug trafficking. He contacted me when I was in med school. He was in trouble and looking for money. We've been in touch off and on since then." Kelsey just stared at him for what felt like hours. Her face was unreadable. "How long have you known this?"

"Before I came to Golden Shores."

She looked at him with disbelief before she jumped up and scowled down at him. "And you've said nothing!"

"I couldn't. I made a promise."

"A promise! How could you keep this from me? I thought you knew how screwed up my family is over what happened to Chad. Not knowing if he was dead or alive. Couldn't you see China's reaction to you the other night?"

Jordon stood. "I made a promise and I take those seriously. I went to visit Chad when I drove down here from Virginia. When I told him I was moving back to Golden Shores he asked me not to tell his family where he was if I ran into any of them. I thought that would never happen. I certainly never dreamed that I would fall in love with his sister."

Kelsey's heart jumped. Her head jerked back, her gaze locking with his. Jordon loved her. Could she trust him to really mean it? "You expect me to believe you love me after you've lied to me for weeks?"

"I've never lied to you. I just didn't speak up." His eyes pleaded with her.

"That's semantics. You expect me to trust you with my heart and life after this? To think I was going to give up my dream job for you!"

"I love you, Kelsey. This isn't the time or place I would've picked to say this but I want to marry you."

"Is that a demand or request? It doesn't matter. What I want to know is if you have been keeping the knowledge that Chad is alive to yourself to use when you had to so that you could keep me in town and in your bed," she spat. "I've wanted out of Golden Shores most of my life. This is my chance and I'm going to take it. Don't try to hold me here by trying to give me what you think I want.

If you care about me you would have told me the minute you knew who I was that my brother was alive."

"I've explained why I didn't. And I don't think you know what you want. You've been running for so long from the loss of Chad, anger at your parents, your reputation as a teen that I don't believe you have any idea what you really want. You were so hurt when Chad left, and me," he said more softly, "you've remained so much that child who was trying to figure out how to get back what she had that you can't recognize what you have in front of you now. You want family around you, that's why you always have to be so involved in planning events.

"All of that is here for you. A sister who loves you and wants you here to help raise your niece or nephew. Parents who I would guess still love you deeply." He put up a hand. "No, don't say it. I know they love you. As an adult I can look back and see that they loved Chad. That's why your father did what he did and your mother agreed. They may not have handled the situation correctly and they made mistakes, like everyone does. You just haven't given them a chance to do any differently. Chad is alive. You can see him for yourself. And you have me heart and soul."

"So what you're saying is Jordon King has ridden in on his shining white horse and tied my world up with a perfect bow?"

Had he sounded that holier than thou? That hadn't been his intent.

His gaze locked with hers. "What I want is your happiness, more than anything else in the world."

"I think if you were that interested in my happiness you would have told me long ago about Chad. Instead of spending so much time trying to fix my life, you might use your time more wisely and work on your own. For all the failings in my family, yours isn't much better. When was the last time you truly spoke to your mother? Maybe you should work on the bow-tying in your own life!"

With that she turned and stalked up the pier toward the house, with Hardy following.

That had gone about as well as he had expected. Except he hadn't thought she'd leave with such a stinging parting shot about his mother. When Kelsey cooled off he'd talk to her again. Make her understand.

He entered the house as she was coming up the hall, pulling her bag and with the wooden box tucked under her arm. "Where're you going?"

She didn't stop as she made the turn toward the kitchen entrance. "To my sister's to let her know that her brother is alive," she hissed, with enough venom to kill if she had bitten.

"Kelsey, don't leave. Let's talk this out." Jordon hated begging. He hadn't even done that when his mother had left.

"Goodbye, Jordon," he heard through the screen door as it slammed shut.

CHAPTER TEN

KELSEY HADN'T WANTED to, had even tried to force herself not to, but she'd cried all the way to China's. This was the first time she'd gone to China in tears in years. When she opened the door to her house Kelsey fell into her arms.

"What's wrong?" China asked, fear etching the words.

"Chad is alive!"

"What?" China let Kelsey go and looked at her. "How do you know?"

"Jordon told me. He's known all along."

"Come in and sit down." China shoved the door closed and pulled Kelsey to the sofa. "Tell me all."

"Chad's in the state prison."

"Chad's alive." China breathed the words. "I can't believe it."

"I can't either."

China threw her arms around Kelsey and hugged her tight. "This is wonderful."

As China let her go she said, "It's wonderful but I just don't understand why Jordon didn't tell us sooner. He should have told us."

"He did tell you."

"Yes, but he has known for weeks. Sat at your table and didn't say anything when we talked about Chad."

"Did he explain why he didn't?"

"He said he promised Chad to keep it a secret."

"So what changed his mind?"

"I don't know. I was so angry I packed my things and left."

China looked at her in disbelief. "Why didn't you ask him?"

Kelsey stopped short. Why hadn't she listened? Because she'd felt like he was being high-handed. Because she had been willing to give up her dream to be with him and he had kept something so important a secret for so long. Because she had been hurt by him before and she was afraid she would be hurt again. Because he'd said things she'd needed to hear but hadn't wanted to. All of the above. Bottom line, she was scared. Scared of life, scared of loving him, scared she'd never find the happiness she'd once had.

But over the last few days with Jordon she'd felt that bliss again. "I don't know," she answered China. But she did.

"We need to tell Mother and Daddy." China stood. "But we can't tonight because they're out of town until Wednesday. We have to come up with the best way to do it between now and then. It'll be such a shock."

"You can tell them."

"Kelsey, this is something we have to do together. It's time you were part of the family, good or bad," China said in the firmest voice Kelsey had ever heard her use. "Come on, you look awful. Stay the night or as long as you need to."

Kelsey went to her car and retrieved her bag and box. She climbed the steps to the door with shoulders hunched like the wrung-out woman she was. Not since Chad had left had her emotions been so shattered. All she wanted to do was curl into a ball, close her eyes and forget.

* * *

Hours later Jordon had no choice but to haul himself out of the recliner to get ready to go to work. He headed to his room. He hadn't gone there last night, knowing the smell of Kelsey and the memories would only make his heartache more painful. Kelsey's negligée lay neatly across his bed. His agony grew as if he had been stabbed with a knife and had it twisted in his chest. The silky material was just as empty as his life would be without her.

The peace he had found by moving back to Golden Shores had disappeared like the summer crowds. Now he was at work glassy-eyed from lack of sleep. Thank goodness it was a busy day, leaving him little time to dwell on Kelsey. A number of times he'd opened charts to see her notes. Disgusted with himself for letting something as small as her initials affect him, he'd click the charts from the screen as soon as he'd been able to.

That afternoon he'd been walking down the hall toward Mr. Sanchez's room. His heart had jerked to a stop for a second when Kelsey had come out of the patient's room along with a woman Jordon assumed was the translator. Glancing at him, Kelsey had said something to the woman beside her, turned, pulled the door to the stairwell open and had been gone. He'd been crushed. Things were so bad between them that Kelsey couldn't bring herself to face him.

He was as lost and angry as he had been when his mother had left. This time he couldn't disappear into drugs and a wild time. He had to face the situation. But could he really do that when he couldn't have a simple conversation with his mother? Had Kelsey been right? Shouldn't he see about his own life before he started messing in hers? Was it time for him to start mending the bridges between him and his mother?

Jordon looked out the windshield at his empty and

lonely bungalow. How had he let his happiness become dependent on Kelsey being in his life? She consumed it. Even Hardy, who lumbered out to meet him instead of running and jumping, seemed as depressed as he was over the absence of Kelsey. It was time he did something about the situation. Past time to start getting his own house in order. He would call his mother.

Half an hour later, with his heart beating fast and with shaking hands he'd never admit to, Jordon punched his mother's number into his phone. He didn't know why but years ago he had saved it in his phone. Had he subconsciously known that one day he would want it?

A voice that was familiar yet different, happy in some way he couldn't explain, answered the phone.

"Mother, it's Jordon."

"Jordon!" The excitement in her voice was almost tangible.

"Mother, why did you do it?"

There was a pause. "Honey, I wasn't happy," she said softly. "I handled things all wrong. I should have been honest with your daddy, with you, but I was scared. I'm so sorry that I hurt you. That you had to carry the burden of knowing for so long. I stayed because I hoped I'd change. Instead, I made it worse for you and your daddy.

"He loved you." Jordon couldn't keep the bitterness out of his voice.

"I know he did. But I just didn't love him back the same way he loved me." She paused then said, "Our hearts don't always let us take the easy road."

He knew that all too well.

"You were a horrible wife, but I realize now that you had been a good mother."

"Thank you for that, Jordon. You don't know how much

that means to me. Not having you in my life has been my greatest regret. I never intended to hurt you."

"Why would you think that having an affair, breaking Daddy's heart and leaving wouldn't have hurt me?"

"Sometimes people make mistakes. Big and small. Mine was big."

Had she said this before and he just hadn't listened or hadn't wanted to? He could understand making mistakes. He'd made them as a teen, professionally and again with Kelsey.

"Jordon, I've miss you."

"I've missed you too." To his surprise, he meant it.

"I'd like to see you some time."

"I'm not ready for that."

"I understand." The disappointment and pain were loud and clear in her voice.

"I'll call."

"Thank you for that, Jordon."

"Bye, Mother."

Kelsey sat in the middle of the bed in the crisp white room that was the direct opposite of the dark emotions that swirled within her.

Her treasure box lay open. She held Chad's picture. The yellow plastic ring was on her finger. She couldn't seem to get past the idea that Jordon had kept such an important secret from her. The one time she'd let a man into her heart and he had disappointed her.

In the next few days she would need to make a major decision. She'd received the phone call she'd hoped for today. The job in Atlanta was hers, if she wanted it. To her astonishment, she hadn't told them immediately that she'd take it. Falling in love with Jordon had taken the luster off the idea of moving away. She was letting a man control her life, something she'd sworn she'd never do again after getting out from under her father's thumb.

A soft knock came at the door and Kelsey said, "Come in."

China entered. "I just wanted to check on you. You came home, headed straight in here and haven't come out. I was getting worried about you. Are you hungry?"

A slight smile teased the corner of her mouth. "Ever the mother. That baby is going to be so spoiled."

"I sure plan to. But right now I'm concerned about you." China sat on the edge of the bed. "Is that a picture of Chad?"

"I stole it out of the photo album." Kelsey handed it to China.

"I'm not surprised. I remember when this was taken." She put the picture down on the bed and picked up Kelsey's hand and touched the piece of plastic circling her finger. "You love him, don't you?"

"Yes, but I don't want to."

"I've been there, done that. But then you find out that you'd rather forgive them than live without them."

"I'm not there yet."

"You will be. I just hope you don't wait too long."

"I got the job offer in Atlanta."

"You did?" China's face remain emotionless. "What did you tell them?"

"That I'd let them know in a few days."

"I think that was wise. I spoke to Mother and Daddy. They're expecting us Wednesday evening."

"You told them I was coming? I bet Daddy is blowing a gasket."

China gave wry smile. "No, I said it would be Payton and I. They would know something was wrong if I said you were coming."

Wednesday afternoon Kelsey rode with Payton and China to her parents' house. She wasn't sure she would have made it if she hadn't been with them. More than once she'd wanted to back out. The only reason she hadn't was because it was time for her to start facing her past and the issues with her parents was a large part of that past.

"What's he doing here?" she said, when she saw Jordon's SUV sitting alongside the road in front of her parents'. She'd not seen him in the last three days outside that one time in front of Mr. Sanchez's room. Not proud of herself for it, she had hidden in her office most of the time, handling the majority of her work over the computer. If she needed to see patients, she did it when she thought Jordon would be having lunch or seeing patients elsewhere. The hospital was small but became tiny when trying to dodge someone.

"I asked him to come," China said. "He should be here to answer any questions Mother and Daddy have. We have."

"I don't want to see him." Even to her own ears she sounded childish. He'd said some things she hadn't wanted to admit were accurate. She needed to deal with Chad being alive. Then she'd figure out how to handle her feelings for Jordon. She was in emotional overload.

"That's not true," China said with the patience of a mother settling a willful child. She was right, but Kelsey wasn't willing to admit it out loud. In truth, she wanted to run to him, bury her head in his strong shoulder and hide. But she had been hiding for too long, from too many problems.

Payton pulled the new minivan to a stop in the drive. Kelsey opened the door to find Jordon standing nearby. He looked haggard, as if he hadn't slept in days, maybe even a little thinner.

It had been at least ten years since she'd been in her parents' home. The thought of facing them was staggering. She stumbled as they walked along the shell drive. Jordon's hand at her elbow steadied her then was gone.

China led the way up the length of steps to the front door of the home built on stilts. Payton followed her then Kelsey.

Jordon moved closer as they climbed and whispered, "I know you don't want me here. I also know how tough it is for you to face your parents. I'm here for you if you need me."

Before Kelsey could form a response her mother opened the door. She bit her lip and her hands shook. As if time had rolled back, Kelsey was once again the young girl who only wanted her mother to show she cared. Jordon stood close enough that she felt heat from his body.

"Well, what's all this?" Her mother scanned the group. A look of shock covered her face when she gaze rested on her. "Kelsey." The wistful note in her mother's voice almost brought tears to Kelsey's eyes.

"Mom, we need to talk to you and Father," China said.

"What's wrong?" Kelsey's mom's face turned anxious.

"Nothing. It's good news."

"Come in." She led them into the living area where her father sat in his favorite spot in front of the TV. Apparently little had changed.

Jordon took a seat next to Kelsey on the sofa. China sat beside her on the opposite side. Payton stood like a protective warrior beside China.

Her father looked straight at Kelsey. "What're you doing here?"

"Good to see you too, Father."

Jordon shifted so that his thigh came in contact with hers. She appreciated the reassurance.

"And who are you?" He looked directly at Jordon.

"I'm Jordon King."

"King." He rolled the name around his mouth. "I know that name. Did you used to live around here?"

China rose. "Let me turn the TV off."

"I was watching a show," her father groused.

Payton put his hand on China's shoulder. "I'll get it."

Kelsey watched in amazement as Payton walked to the TV and pushed a button. Her father said nothing.

"I know you now. You're that King kid that got Chad in trouble." Her father put the foot of the recliner down as if intending to come after Jordon.

To his credit Jordon's voice remained calm as he said, "Yes, I was Chad's friend."

"How dare you come into my house?" Her father moved to stand.

"You need to hear Jordon out," Payton said.

"I don't want to hear anything from him," her father growled.

Payton returned to his spot behind China and she said, "Chad is alive."

"What?" Her mother sat on the edge of her seat.

"It's true, Mrs. Davis," Jordon said.

"Why should we believe you?" Her father continued to scowl at Jordon.

Jordon ignored him and continued. "Chad's in the state prison on drug charges." Her mother groaned but Jordon went on to tell them how he'd come to know where Chad was. "He's fine but has a few more years to serve."

"Chad's alive," her father whispered, as if the truth had finally sunk in. Her father leaned back in his chair. He looked at them. "I did the best I knew how with the boy. It was my job to teach him right from wrong. He had to learn." He look at each of them in turn as if for confirmation he'd done the right thing.

To her amazement there were tears in his eyes.

Her father hung his head. His shoulders jerked. He was sobbing. She watched in shock. Going to her father, her mother put an arm across his shoulders and hugged him.

"I know this is too late but I have never forgiven myself for how I drove him from this house," he said between sniffs. "I was doing what I thought was right at the time."

"That didn't make it hurt less," Kelsey said.

"I know you girls were hurt by my decisions, especially you, Kelsey. I couldn't let Chad hurt our family."

"Yeah, but instead of it just being Chad hurting the family it was you too."

"I know that now. I'm truly sorry for what I've done to this family."

Kelsey wouldn't have thought it possible but she felt sorry for the broken man before her. He'd been big and imposing all her life and now she saw him as a sad, aging man who had hurt like the rest of them.

Her mother looked at Jordon. "Will Chad see us?"

"I think he will. He didn't want me to tell you where he was because he was ashamed. You'll have to call the prison to see when you can visit. I think he'll be glad to see you all. Mr. Davis, I'm sorry for any part you think I played in Chad leaving. I was a kid with my own problems."

Kelsey felt for that scared kid who hadn't known how to handle his life any more than she had known how to handle hers.

"So how do you know my daughters?" her mother asked.

"I'm a doctor at Golden Shores Regional. I have moved back here. Kelsey and I work together."

She needed to get out of there. They had done what

she'd come for. She needed to get away from her father and away from Jordon. Her whole world was squeezing in on her. She had to figure out where she went from here.

"I need to go." Kelsey stood and Jordon did also.

He looked at China. "I'll take care of her."

Kelsey didn't glance right or left on her way to the door. Her mother beat her there.

"You will come back soon, won't you?" Her mother gave her a pleading look.

"I don't know."

"He has changed over the last few months. Knowing Chad is alive will make even more of a difference. He's carried such a burden of guilt over Chad, over you. Maybe he'll become more like the man I married now. He loves you, Kelsey. He didn't know how to show it all the time."

"I know that now, Mom. But I can't forgive all the years of injury all in one day. Give me time."

"We would love to see you any time."

In an impulsive move Kelsey wrapped her arms around her mother and hugged her. Her mother returned the embrace. It felt wonderful being in her mother's arms again.

"Thank you so much, Dr. King," her mother said, as Jordon followed Kelsey out.

"I'm glad I had good news."

As she went down the steps, Kelsey said over her shoulder, "I don't need you to take care of me."

"I know you don't but I want to."

Jordon said the words in such a calm voice she gritted her teeth not to snap at him. She looked up at him when she reached the ground. He stood two steps above and towered over her. This wasn't her best ground for defense but she forged ahead. "I can't do this right now. I can't handle you and my parents in the same day."

"Okay."

"That's all you've got to say?"

He shrugged. "How about where would you like me to drive you?"

Kelsey blinked and looked around. She'd forgotten she'd ridden out with China and Payton.

"You can take me…" The reality that she had no house and no key to China's home left her in confusion.

"Come on, we'll ride around for a while until China and Payton return home. I know you don't want to go back in there and I sure don't." He started toward his SUV.

Kelsey looked back at her parents' door then at Jordon's back. She had no choice but to take the least of the two evils. "I don't want to talk."

"Okay."

Jordon didn't even open the door for her. Instead he climbed in on the driver's side and waited patiently while she joined him. He started the vehicle and pulled on to the road. Kelsey had never been more exhausted in mind, body and soul. She closed her eyes and slipped into sleep.

Jordon turned the engine off and looked at Kelsey. She was so beautiful but more than that she was remarkable in so many ways. People loved her and she loved furiously in return. It must have taken all she'd had to enter her parents' house, having been gone so long. She'd held herself together admirably. If he'd not known her so well he would never have noticed the slight tremor to her hands or seen the flinch she'd made when her father had questioned why she was there. For once in his life he'd wanted to hit an older man.

Kelsey's hair was standing on end in her preferred style that so suited her little left-of-center personality. Her lips were parted and he wanted to lean across and kiss her awake, beg her to see reason. His desire to touch her, do something as simple as run the tip of his finger across her cheek almost took control of him. He climbed out and closed the door behind him. Kelsey needed rest and time then they would talk. He had to get her to listen.

Jordon climbed the steps to the front entrance of the house. He'd seen the look on Kelsey's face. She'd loved the place. He'd put down earnest money on it the day before because the real estate woman had said someone else was interested in it. If he couldn't convince Kelsey that staying in Golden Shores with him was the thing to do, he would willingly forfeit the money and live wherever she wanted.

He ambled from empty room to empty room without paying much attention to where he was. Ending up in the spacious window-filled living area that stretched across the back of the house, he opened the full-length glass door and walked out onto the porch. He glanced at the screen porch then strolled to the dock. Going to the gazebo, he sat on one of the benches and put his head in his hands.

"Hey. I've been looking everywhere for you."

The sound of Kelsey's voice had him jerking upright.

"What're you doing out here? More to the point, what are we doing here?" She gestured toward the house.

"The real estate woman gave me the key so I could look around again."

"So you've decided this is the one?" Her voice had a wispy note that gave him hope.

"It depends."

She came to stand in the entry way of the gazebo. "On what?"

"On you."

"Me? Why?"

"Because I can only live here if you share it with me."

"Jordon, I thought we weren't going to go into all of that now."

He shrugged. "You're the one who asked."

"I guess I did."

Jordon captured her gaze. "I know you don't want to talk but would you be willing to listen for a minute?"

She sighed. "I guess you won't take no for an answer."

"This is something you really need to hear or I wouldn't insist."

She sat down on the bench closest to the opening as if she wanted to make sure she had an escape route. "Okay, I'm listening."

Kelsey was going to be a tough sell. He had hoped she'd softened some over the last few days but apparently not. "When I found out my mother was having an affair I swore then that I would always keep my promises. That trust was the most important thing in a relationship. Because of that I couldn't tell you or your family about Chad. It was too ingrained, too important to who I am to break a promise. I refuse to be like my mother and hurt someone by not keeping my word. But that didn't happen. I did hurt you. I'm sorry for that, but if I had to do it over again I would make the same decision. I hope you can understand why I did what I did."

She just looked at him. Why didn't she say something? At least she wasn't walking off.

"Thank you for telling me. I can't say it still doesn't hurt to know you lied to me."

"If you'll forgive me, I promise that it'll never happen again."

"I guess I can accept that, knowing how strongly you stand by your word."

"Thank you." Relief flooded him. Boosted by her positive reaction and the fact she'd not walked away yet, he asked, "So are you going to take the job?"

Her eyes narrowed. "How do you know they offered me the job? Did China tell you?"

"No. I just know they would be crazy not to want you."

Her lips curled a little before she said, "They do want me."

"So when are you leaving?"

She hesitated a second. "I'm not sure that I am. I told them I needed a few days to think about it."

His heart lightened, hope soared. "Why's that?"

"I wanted to make sure I'm making the move for the right reasons. I have spent so many years planning a way out of Golden Shores that I haven't stopped to think in a long time why I wanted to leave."

He propped his elbows on this knees, trying to give a nonchalant appearance when his happiness hung on her every word. "And do those reasons for leaving still exist?"

' "Yes, but I'm no longer carrying them around like a chip on my shoulder. I've reestablished a relationship with China. I have a job that I love, people I enjoy working with. I did have a place to live."

"You will again."

"Today I faced my biggest fear, seeing my parents again. I survived. You were right, I've been running. I've been planning to for so long it was difficult but freeing to face the past. I can move on now. It isn't where I live, it's who I am. Even if I moved to Atlanta the same issues would follow me. Then China said something to me that made a lot of sense."

Where was she going with this? Dared he dream? He kept his voice even. "That was?"

"Sometimes it's easier to forgive them than to live without them."

"Like your parents?"

"Yeah. But more like you."

"Me?" He croaked then cleared his throat. "What does that mean?"

"It means I love you."

Jordon was on his way to her before she finished the words. Grabbing her, he pulled her against him and brought his mouth down to hers. He poured all his love into that one meeting of lips. Kissing the corner of her mouth, he murmured, "I don't think there has been a man more unhappy than I've been since you left my house. I thought I had lost you."

"It's time I grew up. Time to accept the decisions my parents made. Some that Chad made. I'm not going to live in the past anymore. I want to create a future. Hopefully with you."

Was she really saying all the words he'd dare to hope for? "That can be arranged. Starting right now. I want to do this right this time."

He pulled the circle of gold out of his pocket and went down on one knee.

"Jordon…" Kelsey said his name in that breathy way he adored when he was making love to her.

Kelsey held her breath. Jordon was holding a ring that looked like the plastic one he'd given her so many years ago. But this one glistened in the light. It was made of solid yellow diamonds.

"This came in a smaller box than the last one but I hope you'll accept it anyway. Will you marry me?"

"Oh, just try and stop me!" Kelsey put out her finger and he slipped the ring into place.

EPILOGUE

"KELSEY KING, I thought you got everything you needed yesterday before you left for China's," Jordon said, as they pulled into the drive of their new home.

She leaned over and kissed him. "You already sound like a husband. This won't take but a minute and we really don't have to be at the airport until tomorrow. The hotel room will keep for a few more minutes."

"Speak for yourself. I'm ready for the honeymoon to begin. I missed you last night."

"I missed you too but I bought the dress especially to take to Italy. If I hadn't pulled that casserole out of the oven and gotten a spot on it when I was trying it on we wouldn't have to be doing this."

He chuckled. "I think that's one thing I've enjoyed most about you since you started planning a wedding. You've turned more scatterbrained."

"Scatterbrained? Is that how a new husband should talk about his wife on her wedding day?"

"Maybe not, but it has sure been fun watching you rattled during the last few weeks. Kind of makes me feel loved."

He didn't give her a chance to retort before he climbed out and came around to help her out. Kelsey gathered her full white dress in an arm and Jordon lifted her out of the high SUV.

"The dress is on the porch. I hung it out there to dry."

"While you're getting it I'll double-check that the alarm is set."

"Okay."

Kelsey opened the door to the back porch with a grin on her face. She'd planned this surprise down to the last detail. And Jordon thought her scatterbrained. She'd had the carpenter come in after Jordon had left for the church, Molly's mother had seen to the new luxurious sheets, comforter and pillows. Her father had surprised her by supplying the champagne. "Hey, Jordon, could you come and help me?" she called.

"I'm on my way," he said from the other room. "They say getting married changes you but I had no idea how quickly you would become needy."

Kelsey hurried to get into place on the swing bed inside the screened area of the porch. She lay on her side and adjusted her dress around her.

Jordon stepped out onto the porch. "Now what's the—?"

"Hey, Dr. King, how about you come and start your honeymoon over here on your wedding present," Kelsey called in her most seductive voice.

"When? How? I was just here a few hours ago."

"Instead of asking questions, why don't you kiss me and rock my world?"

He chuckled and came down to join her on the bed. "That I'll be more than happy to do."

Later, with her dress and Jordon's tux lying in a pile on the floor of the porch, Kelsey snuggled under the bedcovers next to Jordon as a light rain fell in the dark.

"You know that if you ever decide you want to live elsewhere else, all you have to do is say the word." Jordon's words rumbled beneath her ear. "I promise."

"And you keep your promises." She shifted so she could look at him. "I don't want to go anywhere. I have everything I've ever wanted right here, J-man."

* * * * *

Mills & Boon® Hardback

September 2014

ROMANCE

The Housekeeper's Awakening	Sharon Kendrick
More Precious than a Crown	Carol Marinelli
Captured by the Sheikh	Kate Hewitt
A Night in the Prince's Bed	Chantelle Shaw
Damaso Claims His Heir	Annie West
Changing Constantinou's Game	Jennifer Hayward
The Ultimate Revenge	Victoria Parker
Tycoon's Temptation	Trish Morey
The Party Dare	Anne Oliver
Sleeping with the Soldier	Charlotte Phillips
All's Fair in Lust & War	Amber Page
Dressed to Thrill	Bella Frances
Interview with a Tycoon	Cara Colter
Her Boss by Arrangement	Teresa Carpenter
In Her Rival's Arms	Alison Roberts
Frozen Heart, Melting Kiss	Ellie Darkins
After One Forbidden Night...	Amber McKenzie
Dr Perfect on Her Doorstep	Lucy Clark

MEDICAL

A Secret Shared...	Marion Lennox
Flirting with the Doc of Her Dreams	Janice Lynn
The Doctor Who Made Her Love Again	Susan Carlisle
The Maverick Who Ruled Her Heart	Susan Carlisle

Mills & Boon® Large Print

September 2014

ROMANCE

The Only Woman to Defy Him	Carol Marinelli
Secrets of a Ruthless Tycoon	Cathy Williams
Gambling with the Crown	Lynn Raye Harris
The Forbidden Touch of Sanguardo	Julia James
One Night to Risk it All	Maisey Yates
A Clash with Cannavaro	Elizabeth Power
The Truth About De Campo	Jennifer Hayward
Expecting the Prince's Baby	Rebecca Winters
The Millionaire's Homecoming	Cara Colter
The Heir of the Castle	Scarlet Wilson
Twelve Hours of Temptation	Shoma Narayanan

HISTORICAL

Unwed and Unrepentant	Marguerite Kaye
Return of the Prodigal Gilvry	Ann Lethbridge
A Traitor's Touch	Helen Dickson
Yield to the Highlander	Terri Brisbin
Return of the Viking Warrior	Michelle Styles

MEDICAL

Waves of Temptation	Marion Lennox
Risk of a Lifetime	Caroline Anderson
To Play with Fire	Tina Beckett
The Dangers of Dating Dr Carvalho	Tina Beckett
Uncovering Her Secrets	Amalie Berlin
Unlocking the Doctor's Heart	Susanne Hampton

Mills & Boon® Hardback

October 2014

ROMANCE

An Heiress for His Empire	Lucy Monroe
His for a Price	Caitlin Crews
Commanded by the Sheikh	Kate Hewitt
The Valquez Bride	Melanie Milburne
The Uncompromising Italian	Cathy Williams
Prince Hafiz's Only Vice	Susanna Carr
A Deal Before the Altar	Rachael Thomas
Rival's Challenge	Abby Green
The Party Starts at Midnight	Lucy King
Your Bed or Mine?	Joss Wood
Turning the Good Girl Bad	Avril Tremayne
Breaking the Bro Code	Stefanie London
The Billionaire in Disguise	Soraya Lane
The Unexpected Honeymoon	Barbara Wallace
A Princess by Christmas	Jennifer Faye
His Reluctant Cinderella	Jessica Gilmore
One More Night with Her Desert Prince...	Jennifer Taylor
From Fling to Forever	Avril Tremayne

MEDICAL

It Started with No Strings...	Kate Hardy
Flirting with Dr Off-Limits	Robin Gianna
Dare She Date Again?	Amy Ruttan
The Surgeon's Christmas Wish	Annie O'Neil

0914GEN STD HB

Mills & Boon® Large Print
October 2014

ROMANCE

Ravelli's Defiant Bride	Lynne Graham
When Da Silva Breaks the Rules	Abby Green
The Heartbreaker Prince	Kim Lawrence
The Man She Can't Forget	Maggie Cox
A Question of Honour	Kate Walker
What the Greek Can't Resist	Maya Blake
An Heir to Bind Them	Dani Collins
Becoming the Prince's Wife	Rebecca Winters
Nine Months to Change His Life	Marion Lennox
Taming Her Italian Boss	Fiona Harper
Summer with the Millionaire	Jessica Gilmore

HISTORICAL

Scars of Betrayal	Sophia James
Scandal's Virgin	Louise Allen
An Ideal Companion	Anne Ashley
Surrender to the Viking	Joanna Fulford
No Place for an Angel	Gail Whitiker

MEDICAL

200 Harley Street: Surgeon in a Tux	Carol Marinelli
200 Harley Street: Girl from the Red Carpet	Scarlet Wilson
Flirting with the Socialite Doc	Melanie Milburne
His Diamond Like No Other	Lucy Clark
The Last Temptation of Dr Dalton	Robin Gianna
Resisting Her Rebel Hero	Lucy Ryder

MILLS & BOON®

Why shop at millsandboon.co.uk?

Each year, thousands of romance readers find their perfect read at millsandboon.co.uk. That's because we're passionate about bringing you the very best romantic fiction. Here are some of the advantages of shopping at www.millsandboon.co.uk:

* **Get new books first**—you'll be able to buy your favourite books one month before they hit the shops

* **Get exclusive discounts**—you'll also be able to buy our specially created monthly collections, with up to 50% off the RRP

* **Find your favourite authors**—latest news, interviews and new releases for all your favourite authors and series on our website, plus ideas for what to try next

* **Join in**—once you've bought your favourite books, don't forget to register with us to rate, review and join in the discussions

Visit **www.millsandboon.co.uk**
for all this and more today!